For Bren,

From or~S.

with

CW01086438

Heathcliff

The Unanswered Questions
Finally Answered?

Sue Barnard

(with some additional material by Emily Brontë)

*"[His history is] a cuckoo's... I know all about it; except
where he was born, and who were his parents, and how
he got his money…"*

(words of Nelly Dean, *Wuthering Heights*, Chapter 4)

CROOKED
CAT

Discover us online:
www.crookedcatbooks.com

Join us on facebook:
www.facebook.com/crookedcat

Tweet a photo of yourself holding
this book to **@crookedcatbooks**
and something nice will happen.

For R.
Love always.

About the Author

Sue Barnard is a British novelist, editor and award-winning poet. She was born in North Wales some time during the last millennium, but has spent most of her life in and around Manchester. After graduating from Durham University she had a variety of office jobs before becoming a full-time parent. If she had her way, the phrase "non-working mother" would be banned from the English language.

Her mind is so warped that she has appeared on BBC TV's *Only Connect* quiz show, and she has also compiled questions for BBC Radio 4's fiendishly difficult *Round Britain Quiz*. This once caused one of her sons to describe her as "professionally weird". The label has stuck.

Sue speaks French like a Belgian, German like a schoolgirl, and Italian and Portuguese like an Englishwoman abroad. She is also very interested in family history. Her own background is far stranger than any work of fiction; she would write a book about it if she thought anybody would believe her.

Sue lives in Cheshire with her extremely patient husband and a large collection of unfinished scribblings. *Heathcliff* (published on 30 July 2018, to coincide with the bicentenary of the birth of Emily Brontë) is her fifth novel.

Also by Sue Barnard:

The Ghostly Father
Nice Girls Don't
The Unkindest Cut of All
Never on Saturday

Acknowledgements

Once again I am indebted to Laurence & Stephanie Patterson of Crooked Cat Books, for believing in this story and for taking me on for a fifth time. I am particularly grateful to Laurence for his sterling work on the cover art, and to Stephanie for her wonderful advice, support, tact and humour as the manuscript went through the editorial mangle.

Thanks are also due to the many friends, writing buddies and beta-readers who have given much-needed encouragement and vital feedback on the work in progress. The book would be so much less without the help of Ailsa Abraham, Vanessa Couchman, Miriam Drori, John Jackson, Gail Richards, Susan Roebuck, Kay Sluterbeck, Jennifer C Wilson, and all the members of the Manchester Scribes writing group: Pauline Barnett, Jo Fenton, Louise Jones, Karen Moore, Helen Sea, Grant Silk, Claire Tansey and Awen Thornber.

A special mention must go to Karen Brimley (my dear schoolfriend who first gave me the idea for writing the book), Cathy Thomas-Bryant (for her inspired suggestion about one aspect of the plot), and the incomparable Mrs Maureen Hall (the excellent teacher who first introduced me to *Wuthering Heights* when we studied it for O-Level English Literature).

Most important of all, I could not go on writing without the unfailing support of my wonderful husband Bob, my sons Nick and Chris, my mum Barbara, and my brothers and sisters-in-law Cliff, Keith, Bron and Tracey – all of whom not only continue to indulge my crazy passion for writing, but actively encourage it.

Principal Characters

In Yorkshire:

At Wuthering Heights (home of the Earnshaw family):

Heathcliff (born 1764), adopted son of Mr & Mrs Earnshaw
Catherine (Cathy) Earnshaw (born summer 1765), blood daughter of Mr & Mrs Earnshaw
Hindley Earnshaw (born summer 1757), blood son of Mr & Mrs Earnshaw
Hareton Earnshaw (born June 1778), son of Hindley Earnshaw
Nelly Dean (born 1757), housekeeper until 1783 and after 1802
Zillah (age unknown), housekeeper from around 1799 to early 1802
Joseph (elderly), servant

At Thrushcross Grange (home of the Linton family):

Edgar Linton (born 1762), son of Mr & Mrs Linton
Isabella Linton (born late 1765), daughter of Mr & Mrs Linton
Cathy Linton (born March 1784), daughter of Edgar Linton
Nelly Dean (as above), housekeeper from 1783 to 1802

Thomas Braithwaite, coachman
Charles Lockwood, tenant of Thrushcross Grange from October 1801 to January 1802

In Liverpool:

Mary O'Keefe, manager of The Mermaid Tavern
William McDougal, businessman
John Burgess, farmer
Matthew Trelawney, fisherman and sailor

Heathcliff

The Unanswered Questions Finally Answered?

PART ONE

DEPARTURE

(1780)

Gimmerton Village, The Yorkshire Moors

1780

Heathcliff

She said it would degrade her to marry me.

I thought we'd always be together. Cathy is my love, my heart, my soul. But she has betrayed me.

She's going to marry that long tall streak of piss, Edgar Linton. I don't for one second believe that she loves him. I certainly thought she'd have more spirit than to shackle herself to that whey-faced idiot. I've no doubt that he loves her (who wouldn't?), but Cathy loving him? Pah! She's marrying him just because he's rich and handsome – two things which I most definitely am not.

There's no place for me at The Heights any more, and no reason at all for me to stay here. That bastard of a brother of hers has always hated me. If it wasn't for Cathy I'd have been out of there long ago. I cannot live without her – but from now on, I will have to.

So I must go. I have no idea where…

***

Catherine Earnshaw

Oh Heavens, what have I done?

Edgar has asked me to marry him, and I've said yes.

Of course I love Edgar. Almost as much as I love Heathcliff.

I know Heathcliff loves me, too. He's part of my soul. Ever since Father brought him home, he's always been part of my life. I was so sure we'd always be together. So much so that I can't imagine life without him.

I love him so much, but he has no money and no prospects. I never thought about it before, until I saw what kind of life I could have if I married Edgar. To marry Heathcliff would be so degrading. We would always be poor. Hindley would never help us; he has always hated Heathcliff. And where would we live? When Hindley dies, The Heights will go to Hareton. What will that mean for me and Heathcliff? Would Hareton take us in out of pity, like poor relations? Even if he did, we would still be beggars.

But if I marry Edgar, I will have a lovely, comfortable home at The Grange.

I do love Edgar. Really, I do. I wouldn't have agreed to marry him otherwise. He's handsome, he's pleasant to be with, he's young and cheerful, and he says he loves me. And he will be rich, and I shall be the greatest woman in the neighbourhood. Of course I love him.

And I'll still have Heathcliff, of course. I will never forsake him. Nothing will ever separate us. Edgar will just have to accept that. And if I marry Edgar I can help Heathcliff to become his own person, out of the reach of Hindley's power.

So why do I feel in my soul as though I'm making a dreadful, dreadful mistake?

I'm going to talk to Nelly. She will know what I must do.

***

Edgar Linton

Catherine has agreed to marry me!

I am the happiest man alive. She is beautiful, spirited and charming, and never in my wildest dreams had I imagined that she would accept me. I had always believed she was in love with that ruffian, Heathcliff. But he is so dreadfully unworthy of her.

Though it pains me to admit this, I will remain eternally

6

grateful to the dog who bit her when the two of them came snooping round The Grange. I hate to think of her being hurt, but if Skulker had not attacked her, she would not have been forced to spend time at The Grange, recuperating. During that time, dear Isabella transformed her from a tomboyish ragamuffin into a fine, genteel lady. Mother and Father came to adore her. They will be thrilled that she has consented to be my wife.

It will be difficult, of course, to persuade her to forsake Heathcliff – but I must try. I will do my utmost to make her happy, and give her no cause whatsoever to pine for him or to regret her decision to marry me.

But we will not be married for quite a while, so I should have plenty of time.

***

Nelly Dean

I really don't understand what Miss Catherine can be thinking of. The only possible explanation is that she must have lost her mind.

Earlier this evening, she came to see me in the kitchen, almost in tears. During the afternoon, whilst Mr Edgar was visiting her, she behaved appallingly towards me and young Hareton, and she even slapped Mr Edgar's face. Goodness only knows what he must have thought of her. When she first appeared I wondered if she might have come to say she was sorry, though I'm well aware that this is not in her nature.

What she did say almost knocked me sideways. She told me that Mr Edgar has asked her to marry him, and that she has accepted! Then – incredibly – she asked me if she was doing the right thing.

As if I could give her an answer! But in any case, it certainly isn't my place to tell her. If she really is doing the right thing by marrying Mr Edgar, she would know in her own heart, and wouldn't need to ask anyone – let alone the likes of me.

I asked her if she loves Mr Edgar. She said she does,

7

because he's "handsome, and pleasant, and young, and cheerful, and rich." And also because he loves her.

My first thought, on hearing this, is one which I would rather not repeat. My second thought was *Heaven help poor Mr Edgar*... I managed to control myself and tried to reason with Miss Catherine, suggesting that she might be marrying him for all the wrong reasons.

But even though I could see she was already beginning to have doubts about it (she even admitted that in her heart and her soul she was convinced she was wrong), she wouldn't listen to me. Not that I'm surprised. She was always a wilful and headstrong thing, even as a child.

Then she told me that she'd once dreamed she was in Heaven, but she'd been so miserable that the angels had thrown her back down to earth. It made me feel very uneasy, to be honest, until she explained that she had no more business to be in Heaven than she had to marry Mr Edgar.

But then she said, "It would degrade me to marry Heathcliff."

I was so taken aback at this that at first I failed to notice a slight sound from behind the settle, and possibly the creak of a door. I glanced up, and imagined I saw a faint movement in the shadows. But Miss Catherine, who was sitting on the floor with her back to the door, went on talking.

If I thought she was crazy before, what she said next convinced me of it. Her next words, after saying it would degrade her to marry Heathcliff, were "...so he shall never know how I love him".

Oh dear God in Heaven.

I opened my mouth to say: "Love is a great leveller, Miss Catherine. So if you really love Heathcliff, then the question of rank or status wouldn't, or shouldn't, enter into it." But before I could speak she just carried on, saying her soul and Heathcliff's were one and the same, whereas hers and Edgar's were as different as they could possibly be.

Yet another reason why marrying Mr Edgar is the worst thing she could possibly do.

When she finally paused for breath I held up my hand for

silence, saying I'd heard the sound of Joseph's cart in the yard, and it was likely that Heathcliff would be with him. At that point, she panicked, clearly terrified that Heathcliff might have any suspicion of what she's done.

"But Heathcliff doesn't know anything about love, does he, Nelly?" she declared.

"How can you be so sure of that, Miss Catherine?" I replied. "Is there any reason why he shouldn't know? Let's just suppose that he does – and that you might be the one he loves. Can you even begin to imagine how he might feel, once he finds out that you're going to marry Edgar Linton?"

"But we'll still be together," she protested. "Don't you understand, Nelly? Nobody will ever separate us! Edgar will understand, once he realises how much Heathcliff means to me."

My face must have betrayed my horror at this point, because she carried on: "Nelly, I know you must think I'm a selfish brat. But has it not occurred to you that if I married Heathcliff, we'd be little more than beggars? Whereas if I marry Edgar, I can help Heathcliff to better himself."

I was aghast. "With your husband's money, Miss Catherine? Do you honestly think you can get away with that? And, begging your pardon, I think that's your worst reason yet for agreeing to marry Mr Edgar."

"No, it is the best reason of all!" she shouted. "Don't you see how unselfish I'm being? I'm doing this for Heathcliff, not for myself or for Edgar! Don't you understand?"

"No, Miss Catherine, I'm afraid I don't understand." By now I had run out of patience with her. "As far as I can tell, either you have no idea of what is expected of a married woman, or you are just a spoilt, unprincipled child. Please spare me any more of your ramblings."

At this point the door opened and Joseph entered, effectively bringing our conversation to a close. Miss Catherine slumped into a seat in the corner, whilst I moved to the stove to continue preparing the supper. As I passed round to the other side of the settle, I spotted a small pale object on the floor underneath the bench by the wall. Bending down to retrieve it, I recognised Heathcliff's clay pipe.

I recalled having heard the door creak. That was when I realised what had happened: Heathcliff must have overheard the earlier part of our conversation, up to when Miss Catherine said it would degrade her to marry him – at which point, he'd got up and left.

After we'd finished eating, Joseph asked where Heathcliff was.

"What?" Miss Catherine asked, visibly alarmed. "I thought he was out with you."

Joseph grunted and shook his head.

I went out to the barn and called Heathcliff's name, but there was no answer. I searched around the grounds, but he was nowhere to be found.

Returning to the kitchen, I showed Miss Catherine the pipe, and whispered to her that I believed Heathcliff might have overheard much of what the two of us had been saying – or, at least, the first part of it.

Hearing this, she snatched the pipe from my hand and ran outside, frantically shouting and searching for Heathcliff. I tried to reassure her that the clouds looked threatening and that once it started raining he'd soon be back. But even when the storm broke, he did not return.

Miss Catherine stayed outside until long after midnight. By the time we finally persuaded her to come back indoors, she was soaked through and chilled to the bone. And there was still no sign of Heathcliff.

***

Thomas Braithwaite, Coachman

I didn't see the man at first, in the dark and the rain. It was only when he stepped out into the road, a mere few yards in front of the coach, that I saw him at all. I yelled, "Whoa!" and yanked on the reins to slow the horses down. He must have heard me, because he looked up and tried to jump out of the way, but I felt a thud, and heard a cry of pain.

I pulled the horses to a halt and stepped down from the box

seat. That was when the carriage lamp lit up his face, and I got a better look at him.

It was not a comforting sight. He was lying on the ground and his arm was bleeding. He had no coat, his hair and clothes were soaking wet, and the eyes which were staring up at me displayed a wild light which gave him the appearance of a man possessed.

"Is anything the matter, sir?" I ventured to ask – although I knew the answer to this question almost before it had left my lips. Even without the injury to his arm, I could tell that there was clearly something very much the matter. No man in his right mind would be wandering across the moors, coatless and hatless, on a wet and blustery night such as this.

He stared at me and staggered to his feet, all the while muttering under his breath. As he drew nearer I could hear that he was making the same sound over and over again. But it made no sense. It sounded like "Degrade… degrade… degrade…"

I walked towards him, extending my hand.

"Sir, you are injured, and it is not good to be out in this foul weather. Please, will you allow me to transport you to your home?"

"Home?" he snarled, baring his teeth. "I have no home. Not now."

I was anxious to know what had brought him hither, in a temper which so strongly matched the tempest around us – but this was neither the time nor the place to ask. Instead, I hastily tied my kerchief around the wound in his arm, then gestured towards the coach and offered to transport him to the nearby inn which was to be the coach's destination for the night.

He appeared to consider this for a moment, then shrugged his thick-set shoulders and gave a barely perceptible nod.

I opened the coach door and motioned him to climb aboard. As he entered, I heard various words from the other passengers within, but could not make out what was being said. I closed the door behind him, climbed back into the box seat and tugged on the reins. The horses broke into a canter as we covered the remaining few miles to the inn.

I was troubled. Who was this mysterious stranger, and what was he fleeing from?

***

Catherine Earnshaw

Nelly has just told me that I should have refused Edgar's proposal. She said that if he'd asked me after seeing the way I'd behaved this afternoon, he must be (to use her own words) "either hopelessly stupid, or a venturesome fool".

She thinks I'm marrying Edgar for all the wrong reasons. She didn't believe me when I said I loved him. I gave her all my reasons for loving him, but she still failed to understand. She said that the fact that he loves me should count for nothing, as I ought to love him regardless of that – and that without his handsome looks and cheerful manner I would probably not love him in any case.

That much is true, I grant her; if Edgar were ugly and boorish I have no doubt that I would hate him – or pity him, at the very least. She even said that he will not always be young and handsome, and may not always be rich. What utter nonsense!

And she doesn't understand about Heathcliff, either. She tried to suggest that if Heathcliff loves me, it would break his heart if I married Edgar. But what does Heathcliff know about love?

Then, when I told her about my plans to help Heathcliff after I was married, she said that I had no idea of what being married should mean, and that I was wicked and unprincipled. She even said that helping Heathcliff by using my husband's money was the worst possible motive for marrying Edgar!

Well, I'm going to marry Edgar in any case, whether Nelly likes it or not.

But right now, that is the very least of my worries. Nelly has just told me that she thinks Heathcliff might have heard us talking earlier. And now he has disappeared.

***

Later, once we were settled at the inn, I joined the stranger by the fire. His arm now bore a stronger bandage, which appeared to have done a better job of staunching the bleeding. His clothes and hair looked a little less sodden, and with his good hand he was puffing on a clay pipe, which I recognised as one from the pot on the bar. An empty tankard sat forlornly on the table in front of him.

"Another drink?" I asked.

"Thanks," he grunted. He appeared slightly less morose now, possibly due to the effects of the ale, and the fact that he was no longer at the mercy of the elements. Looking at him more closely, I was surprised to see that he was much younger than I had first thought – no more than sixteen or seventeen at the most.

I took his tankard and my own to the innkeeper and returned with them brim-full. The stranger nodded his thanks, laid aside his pipe and took a large swig.

"Where are you travelling to?" I ventured to ask, after having slaked my own thirst.

"I have no idea," he growled. "I just need to get away from here."

I was unsure how to answer this, but was spared the need to reply as the stranger spoke again.

"I've just heard the girl I love tell someone that it would degrade her to marry me. She's promised to marry some rich spoilt brat who has all the charm of a household slopbucket."

It would degrade her? That, at least, would explain what he'd been saying when I found him on the moor.

He took another mouthful of his ale. "Where is the coach going tomorrow?"

"To Liverpool. We leave at first light."

He looked up in surprise when I mentioned Liverpool, as though this held some significance for him. He was silent for a moment, then appeared to make a decision.

"Is there space for one more?"

"I should think so. I'm not expecting any more passengers."

He nodded, drained his tankard, then rose to his feet.

"In that case, I will bid you good night, and will see you at first light tomorrow."

***

Heathcliff

I was very nearly run over by the coach. As it was, I escaped with a few bruises and a cut to my arm.

The coach has taken me as far as an inn on the edge of the moors, where it stopped for the night. The coachman insisted that I should come with them, as he was concerned about my injury. The innkeeper's wife also took pity on me, giving me some hot broth and a mug of spiced ale before offering me a cheap room in the rafters.

During the evening, I spoke briefly with the coachman as we sat by the fire in the bar-room. He told me that the coach is going to Liverpool, and will leave at first light in the morning to continue its journey westwards. He has agreed to let me travel with them.

I have very little memory of my life before old Mr Earnshaw brought me to The Heights, but I do remember him telling me that he first found me on the streets of Liverpool. How strange that fate has conspired to send me back there.

There is still some way to go, and I have very little money left after paying for my night's accommodation here. But I must go on; I cannot go back to The Heights now.

***

Edgar Linton

I have just heard that Heathcliff has disappeared from The Heights, and nobody knows where he has gone. I must confess that I am relieved to hear this news, although Catherine is distraught. This worries me somewhat, as it suggests that her feelings for him still run deep, and it will be difficult to persuade her that perhaps all has turned out for the best...

***

14

The following morning, the stranger joined me in the stable yard as the other passengers began to take their places in the coach.

"How is your arm?" I asked him.

"Still sore, but it's not broken. I think I will live." I detected a faint ghost of a grin on his face as he spoke. "May I sit on the box seat with you? I don't think the other passengers will want my company again today."

"Are you sure?" I answered, surprised at his request. "Won't it make your arm worse?"

He grunted. "Even if it does, I'd rather have your company than sit inside. My intrusion last night was quite clearly not welcome. And in any case, I hate being confined. Certainly not with snobs like them." He glanced towards the gloomy interior of the coach and grimaced.

"Very well." I was unsure of the wisdom of this, but he seemed determined, and I had no wish to incur his wrath by arguing with him. Our acquaintance, brief though it had been, had already shown me that he was not a man who would suffer fools gladly.

As we set off, he looked around at the moors surrounding us.

"It is a long time since I was last in Liverpool," he muttered, as much to himself as to me.

"How long?"

"More than ten years. I was only a child when I left."

"So what brought you to Yorkshire?"

"Not so much 'what' as 'who'. I was brought here by the master of the house I have just left."

I was puzzled. "Why?"

"I'm not sure. Out of the kindness of his heart, I think. He'd come to Liverpool for something to do with his business – I don't know what exactly – and he found me wandering and begging on the streets. He brought me back to Yorkshire with him, and it's been my home ever since. Until last night." He relapsed into gloom as he spoke the last three words.

15

I was silent as I recalled his revelation of the previous evening.

Then he spoke again. "He carried me here, all the way, inside his great-coat."

"What? Even in the stagecoach?"

Now it was his turn to look surprised. "Stagecoach? No, not at all. He walked the whole way."

***

Catherine Earnshaw

Oh Heavens, what has happened to Heathcliff? He hasn't been seen since yesterday evening. I waited outside for him until long after midnight in the hope that he would come home. And now I feel so cold…

***

Thomas Braithwaite, Coachman

"When we first arrived at the house," the stranger went on, "Mr Earnshaw – that's the man who found me – handed me to his wife. As I recall, she didn't seem to be very happy about having another child in the house. But he insisted, and told her that they would name me 'Heathcliff'. This was the name of a son of theirs who'd died some years earlier. They had two other living children: a boy called Hindley and a girl called Catherine."

His voice wavered as he said her name. I wondered if this 'Catherine' might be the girl who had so recently broken his heart.

"She was the same age as me," he went on. "Her brother" (here his voice hardened) "was a a few years older. He took against me right from the start."

"Why was that?" I asked.

"To begin with, it was because he'd asked his father to bring him a fiddle back from Liverpool, and it had got crushed in the folds of the great-coat as he'd been carrying me. Then, afterwards, he got it into his head that his father preferred me to him."

"And did he?"

"I don't know. But Mr Earnshaw certainly treated me like a son. Hindley hated that, but his father sent him away to school, and after that life got much easier. But when the old man died – that was three years ago – Hindley inherited the house and came back to run it. That was when things really started to go wrong. He stopped all my lessons with the curate, made me live with the servants, and forced me to work on the farm like a common labourer."

"What about Catherine?" I asked.

"What about her?" His voice was expressionless.

"Did she treat you badly too?"

He paused before answering. "Not in that way," he said eventually, in a voice so low that I could barely discern the words.

"But in another way?"

"Yes. In the worst way possible. She betrayed me."

"So – was she the girl you told me about when we spoke yesterday evening?"

He nodded. "My Cathy. I love her to death."

His tone made me shudder. Whose death did he have in mind? His own, or hers, or someone else's?

17

PART TWO

ADVENTURE

(1780-1783)

Liverpool

1780

Mistress Mary O'Keefe, manager of The Mermaid Tavern, Liverpool

Well, that was a strange evening, and no mistake.

It started out ordinarily enough – the usual crowd came in and started planning their next moves. Mr McDougal said that he'd heard news of a new convoy of ships heading for the Americas, and there were rumours that they'd be carrying cargo of French brandy, and gin and lace from the Low Countries. Rich pickings, I'd say. Not to mention the sugar. I have lots of recipes for cakes and the like; all very good for using up the stuff so that those dastardly revenue men don't sniff it out.

Well, anyway, they were all sitting in their usual corner, drinking their tankards of ale and smoking their pipes, when the door opened and in walked a total stranger. I could tell he wasn't from these parts, because he spoke with a strange twang in his voice. And he looked dark and swarthy, almost foreign-looking. If it wasn't for the way he spoke, I'd swear there might even be a touch of the Irish gypsy about him.

But he was tall, quite young, and looked very strong. Mr McDougal bade him welcome, and bought him a pint of ale. He was gruff and brusque at first, but nonetheless he sat down at the table with them. I offered him a bite to eat, and he grunted his thanks. It was only a bowl of potage, the heel of a loaf and a lump of hard cheese, but he wolfed it down as though he'd not eaten for days. Well, maybe he hadn't, for he cheered up a little once he'd got some food in his stomach.

"What kind of soup is this?" he asked, when he had finished and had wiped the bowl clean with the remains of the bread. "It is quite unlike anything I have ever tasted."

"I call it mock turtle, sir," I replied. "It is made to my own special secret recipe."

He nodded appreciatively. I took away his dish and then offered him a slice of my rich plum cake, which he accepted and devoured with equal gusto. By the time he had finished he was almost smiling.

Then he asked if there was any work going. I could tell that he was down on his luck. Having once touched the depths of despair myself, I could not turn him away.

"Do you need somewhere to stay?" I asked him.

He nodded. "But I cannot afford—"

I held up my hand for silence. "You are welcome to lodge here for the moment. Whilst you search for work you can help me in the tavern, in return for your board and lodging."

"Thank you. You are very kind."

The other men round the table all looked at one another, then Mr McDougal spoke.

"Are you strong, young sir?" he asked.

By way of answer, the stranger rose from his chair and walked over to where I was standing. In an instant he had whisked me off my feet, picked me up as though I weighed no more than a small child, and carried me back to the table.

"Is this strong enough for you?" he asked.

The other men were all clearly impressed.

"Indeed it is!" said Mr McDougal. "Now, pray unhand Mistress O'Keefe and allow her to return to her business."

The stranger complied, setting me down on the ground as swiftly and effortlessly as he had picked me up.

I smoothed my apron and returned, flustered, to my place behind the counter. But I could still follow their conversation.

"Where are you from, young sir?" asked Mr McDougal.

"From Yorkshire," answered the stranger.

"And what, may I ask, brings you here to Liverpool? It is a long way from your home."

"It is no longer my home," the stranger answered, in a voice heavy with both anger and regret.

"Why not?" asked Mr McDougal, carefully.

"I would rather not say at this point," the stranger replied. "But for now, suffice it to say that I have neither desire nor reason to return. I am seeking a new life, far away from the troubles I leave behind."

I caught my breath, and the men around the table all exchanged glances. They were clearly all thinking the same as I was: what kind of life – and what kind of troubles – was this young man leaving behind?

Was he a fugitive from justice? If he was, what crime had he committed? Was there a price on his head? Was he fleeing from the hangman's noose? If so, did he realise that by coming here, he might well be leaping from the frying pan straight into the heart of the fire?

***

Heathcliff

Today the coach took me the remainder of the way to Liverpool. I rode on the box seat with the coachman, who charged me only a few pence for the journey, lengthy though it was. I was deposited by the dockside during the late afternoon, and wandered along the waterfront until I found a tavern, The Mermaid, overlooking the sea. I realised I was hungry and thirsty, so ventured inside in the hope of finding a bite to eat and a measure of ale. By now, I had very little money left, but I hoped I might find something I could afford – or maybe some kind innkeeper who might take pity on me.

The owner of the tavern was a kindly and motherly-looking lady. She served me with a bowl of broth and some bread and cheese, and also asked me if I needed somewhere to stay. I told her that I needed somewhere very cheap, at least until I could find a means of earning some money. She said I was welcome to stay at The Mermaid, and that I could help her in the tavern in return for bed and board.

***

Whatever the stranger's origins or story, he had no time for further discussion – for at that point the tavern door crashed open and young Sam Wallace rushed in.

"Coastguard!" he gasped.

The stranger looked puzzled, but I (and all the other men round the table) understood the warning. One of them immediately pulled a pack of playing cards out of his pocket and began dealing.

Mr McDougal laid a comradely hand on the stranger's arm, and murmured, "We will talk again anon, young sir. But for the moment, please join us in a game of cards, and speak of nothing else except the inclemency of the weather."

The stranger still looked bemused, but then shrugged and complied with Mr McDougal's request. None too soon, for within a minute the door had opened and three men had entered. I recognised them immediately. So, apparently, did all the customers (save the stranger), for the atmosphere inside the tavern changed imperceptibly. An unnatural hush descended over the table, and all the players seemed fixedly intent upon the cards in their hands. Fortunately, the newcomers appeared not to have noticed, absorbed as they were in their need for refreshment.

"Good evening, Mistress O'Keefe," said one of them, placing three tankards on the bar. "Three measures of your finest ale, if you please."

"Of course, gentlemen," I answered, filling the tankards from the brown jug I kept for the purpose. It always amused me that each time they visit my tavern they always refer to my 'finest ale', when in truth all my ale comes from the same barrel. But who am I to question their judgment? After all, their money is just as good as that of my other customers, even though there are some who might not agree with me...

Out of the corner of my eye I noticed a slight disturbance at the card table. All the players suddenly tensed up, and Mr McDougal looked particularly agitated. But the stranger, who was seated alongside him, caught his eye and winked – at which point Mr McDougal and all the others appeared to relax.

I didn't see what happened at the table after that, busy as I was by keeping the new customers occupied at the bar. Once they had all drunk their fill and left, Mr McDougal and the others put away their playing cards and finished their drinks.

After the newcomer (who gave his name as Heathcliff) had retired to his room, Mr McDougal called me to one side and explained what had happened. It transpired that Mr Burgess had dropped his tobacco pouch.

"That man will be the ruin of us all one day," he sighed. "I only keep him on because I can't risk kicking him out. Which reminds me, Mistress O'Keefe, will you please keep your usual eagle eye on young Heathcliff for a few days? I need to make sure he isn't working undercover."

"Of course, Mr McDougal. As always, you can rely on my discretion."

This is not by any means the first time that Mr McDougal had asked me to assess whether someone might be suitable for joining his operations. He knows that I can find out enough to decide if someone can be trusted. '*Nobody will ever suspect a woman,*' he always says.

***

Heathcliff

There were other customers in there, all of whom seemed friendly and welcoming enough. But there was a peculiar incident whilst I was there, involving some visitors – three men – who seemed to be not welcomed by the other customers. The owner, who I discovered was called Mistress O'Keefe, was courteous to them, but the other customers ignored them completely, and even invited me to join them in their collective snubbing of these newcomers. I wasn't quite sure why this should be, but I joined them anyway. We made the pretence of playing a few hands of cards.

One of the other men at the table seemed distant and troubled. For most of the time, he sat staring into space. His mind clearly wasn't on the cards in his hand, and more than once his neighbour had to nudge him to bring his attention back to the game. On one of these occasions he appeared to drop something on to the floor. It looked to me as though he hadn't noticed it, but the others definitely did – and they all tensed up and kept looking nervously at the three men standing at the bar.

At the time I didn't know what it was all about, but I could detect enough to realise that they didn't want those men, whoever they were, to know about the object on the floor. From where I was sitting I could just about make out that it was quite small, so I covered it with my foot, edged it out of sight, and kept it hidden until the men at the bar had drunk their ale, made their farewells and left.

After that, I bent down and retrieved the object – which proved to be a tobacco pouch – and returned it to its owner. He was very grateful, though he didn't appear to know that he'd dropped it in the first place.

Afterwards one of the other men thanked me profusely for what I'd done. It seemed odd that just putting my foot on a tobacco pouch and picking it up again later should seem so significant to him. He asked me what I was doing in Liverpool. I told him I'd only just arrived, and was looking for work. At that point, he looked at me a little quizzically, but then invited me to join them again at The Mermaid the following evening.

**

William McDougal

Tonight at The Mermaid, we were honoured again by a visit from those confounded revenue men. They didn't find anything, of course; the hiding places are too good for them to sniff out, and Mistress O'Keefe was her usual efficient self at keeping their attention diverted on to her 'finest' ales. But we did have a fairly close shave at one point…

Earlier in the evening, a young man appeared at The Mermaid whom none of us had seen before. He had a swarthy, almost foreign-looking air about him. I was briefly reminded of Mistress O'Keefe's Irish gypsy background, and for a moment I wondered if he too was lately arrived from Ireland. But at first he had very little to say for himself, and when he did speak, his voice betrayed a strange accent which was most definitely not of Irish origin.

Then we were interrupted by our 'coastguard' warning which signalled that the revenue men were approaching. We sprang into action with our usual plan: gathering around the table with our tankards of ale and our modest-looking clay pipes, and giving the impression of being absorbed in the seemingly innocent activity of playing a hand of cards. For appearance's sake, I invited the stranger to join us at the card table, but first warned him to keep the conversation to innocent topics such as the weather. He appeared a little puzzled at the request, but seemed willing enough to comply.

The revenue men came in and went over to the bar. Mistress O'Keefe was in the process of filling their tankards when that idiot John Burgess (who I'm sure had had a few too many measures of Mistress O'Keefe's latest brew) dropped his tobacco pouch on to the floor.

The pouch was crammed full of the finest Virginia leaves from our latest haul. If the revenue men had spotted it, there could have been some pretty awkward questions asked; its contents were worth far more than someone of Burgess's meagre means could ever hope to afford.

But the situation was saved by the stranger. Even if he knew nothing of the circumstances, he must all the same have sensed our alarm. He carefully placed his foot so that it lay between the pouch and the revenue men's line of sight, then slowly manoeuvred the pouch out of view under the table and covered it lightly with his other foot.

Once the revenue men had drunk their fill and left us, he retrieved the pouch from the floor and returned it to its owner. Burgess seemed blissfully unaware of how close he had come to unmasking our entire operation.

I bought the stranger a drink to show my thanks for his quick thinking and prompt action. He was a man of few words and surly disposition, but he did say that he had only just arrived in Liverpool.

It was getting late by this stage and we were all looking forward to our beds, so for now, I simply invited him to join us again in the bar tomorrow evening. Mistress O'Keefe has kindly offered to let him stay at The Mermaid, so she can keep an eye on him for a little while. She knows how to figure out if he's working undercover.

Once we're sure he can be trusted, I'll have a proper talk with him and see if he might be suitable for joining our crew. I am sure he will tell me more once I have gained his confidence. He looks like a strong fellow, and no stranger to hard work, so he would make a fine tubman. We shall see…

***

John Burgess

I hope McDougal doesn't have one of his fits of temper after what happened at The Mermaid tonight. I know I've sailed pretty close to the wind in the past, but this time it was very nearly a complete disaster. Some of those damned revenue men turned up, and whilst the rest of us were pretending to play cards I dropped my tobacco pouch.

I was saved by the quick thinking of a young stranger who'd turned up at The Mermaid out of the blue. Somehow – I've no idea how – he noticed what had happened, and covered the pouch with his foot until after the revenue men had gone.

When he handed it back to me I thanked him, and pretended I hadn't realised what had happened. But the truth is that I was too afraid to admit to what I'd done. If McDougal thinks I'm not up to the task, he won't think twice about getting rid of me, and if I lose the job with the gang I don't know what we'll do. It's difficult enough trying to keep one step ahead of the press gangs. I couldn't face going through all that again.

I haven't told McDougal about little Emily. I've often wondered whether I should, but I don't think he'd understand. He doesn't have much time for other people's problems. But I'm so worried about her. Right now, The Mermaid is my only respite from it all…

***

I've now been staying at The Mermaid for a few days. For the time being, Mistress O'Keefe is allowing me to work in the tavern in return for my board and lodgings. She is very kind, and has a gentle, motherly air about her. It is difficult to tell how old she is, but I would guess she's around the same age as old Mrs Earnshaw would have been if she'd still been alive.

On the second evening, I met with the men again. The one who had invited me to join them introduced himself as William McDougal. He told me he'd come originally from Scotland, but thirty-five years ago, when he was five, he and his mother had been forced to flee after his father was killed at the Battle of Culloden. This, he said, had been a failed attempt to restore the English throne to its rightful Stuart heir ("the King over the Water", he called him). I've never heard anything about this, and, to be honest, it didn't mean very much to me even after he'd explained it. But then, after that brute Hindley stopped my lessons with the curate, there's probably an awful lot more that I don't know.

I told him a bit about myself – how I'd been adopted by a kindly man in Yorkshire, and how life had been pretty good until old Mr Earnshaw died and his son had taken over. I didn't tell him the real reason why I'd left, though. He can go on thinking I left because of Hindley.

McDougal seems very worldly-wise. It also turns out that he's a Catholic. I've never come across Catholics before. Or churches at all, for that matter. We never really bothered with any of that at The Heights – certainly not once Hindley was in charge. He seemed to prefer holy spirit of a rather different kind.

They seem like a very friendly crowd. I wonder what they all do for a living?

***

William McDougal

Well, Mistress O'Keefe seems satisfied that young Heathcliff can be trusted. Maybe the time has now come to see if he's up to the job.

***

Heathcliff

Yesterday evening, McDougal took me to one side. He suddenly seemed much more serious than before.

"Are you still looking for work?" he asked me.

"Mistress O'Keefe has very kindly offered me work at The Mermaid in return for allowing me to stay there," I answered, "but I know I can't impose on her generosity for ever. So, yes, I am. Do you know of anything suitable?"

"Possibly." He looked around, then lowered his voice to a whisper. "Do you remember those men who came to the tavern the evening you first arrived?"

"Yes. What of it? Who were they?"

"They were revenue men."

"What are revenue men?"

McDougal seemed shocked that I didn't know about revenue men, but he explained, "They work for the King, collecting taxes."

"What sort of taxes?"

"All sorts. But mainly taxes on goods brought to this country from elsewhere. It involves a great deal of paperwork." McDougal grinned. "We are kindly folk here, young Heathcliff. We do not like to think of these poor gentlemen having to spend all their time filling in that tedious paperwork, so we like to spare them as much trouble as possible. We describe ourselves as 'free traders', and The Mermaid is our centre of operations. It's full of hiding places there where our goods can be concealed from prying eyes."

"What sort of 'goods' do you – er – trade in?"

"All sorts, but our main commodities are tea, sugar, wine, brandy and tobacco."

"Tobacco?" I recalled the incident from my first evening in

Liverpool. "So, the tobacco in that pouch... had it come from —?"

"Yes. And we have no shortage of customers. The government has always been greedy, but we have no love for them – and the taxes they force on us are much higher now."

"Why is that?"

McDougal sighed. "It's mainly because of the wars. First with France, then with the Americas, and now with the Low Countries. Those thieves in the government have to finance the wars somehow, and it's always the people who end up having to foot the bill. We see it as our duty to save the people as much money as possible. The money is far better in their pockets – or indeed ours – than in the coffers of the Exchequer." Then his voice hardened and his eyes grew steely. "And I have no respect for that German usurper who currently sits on the English throne, nor for anything he represents."

There was a pause whilst I took all this in.

"I see," I said after a moment. "And where do I fit into your plans?"

"It is in the nature of our operations. Although, obviously, our merchandise arrives by sea, much of our – er – enterprise takes place on land. Once the goods have arrived, we need to transport them from the coast to places where they can be safely hidden. Such as here at The Mermaid, for example. But, as I am sure you can appreciate, that is a difficult and often dangerous task. In essence, young Heathcliff, we need strong men to help us transport the goods."

"In that case, Mr McDougal, I am with you. I am well used to hard work, and I have little respect for authority. Especially when that authority is abused." I thought again of Hindley.

McDougal grasped my hand in a firm, brotherly grip, then he described what he had in mind for me. He wants me to join the land gang as a tubman, which (from what I can gather) is some kind of porter.

It's dark now, and I'm just about to go on my first assignment.

***

31

William McDougal

Heathcliff admitted that he was no lover of authority, "especially when that authority is abused" (to use his own words).

He said this with such feeling that I am sure he has had first-hand experience of such abuse. I did not pursue the matter, but I feel sure that he will tell me more once I have come to know him a little better. For my part, I told him my own opinion of the German usurper who currently occupies the English throne.

When pressed to explain why, I told Heathcliff a little of my own background. Heathcliff appeared to know nothing whatsoever about Culloden, or the Jacobites, or 'the King over the Water'. It seems that despite his evident intelligence, his level of education is basic in the extreme.

This may prove to be a good thing, as he might be less likely to ask any awkward questions. At any rate, he seems – so far, at least – to be much more reliable than that idiot, Burgess.

Heathcliff is going to join us for our assignation this evening. It will be interesting to see how he fares.

***

Heathcliff

It is now a little after three o'clock in the morning, and I've just got back to The Mermaid. My back and limbs ache, and I know I ought to try to rest, but my mind is buzzing. I need time to let it slow down before I can sleep.

My first assignment with the gang was simple enough in principle. We assembled on the foreshore and waited, looking out to sea. There was no moon, which McDougal told me would work to our advantage as it would reduce the risk of being detected.

It was not long before a curious blue flash appeared on the horizon, at which point McDougal produced a strange-looking lamp which had a long spout in front of the flame. He looked carefully around, then lit the lamp and pointed the spout towards the open sea. I suppose the flame could be seen from directly in front of McDougal, but it was invisible to anyone standing alongside or behind him. As we waited, he explained to me that the blue flash we had seen had come from a ship which was anchored just out of sight of the land. He had signalled a reply to indicate that the coast was clear, but had used the special lantern (it was indeed called a 'spout lantern') in order to avoid detection. It seems that there are harsh penalties for signalling to ships out at sea.

McDougal's signal, whatever it was, must have been successful, because a few minutes later a small rowing boat appeared out of the darkness. It was loaded with bales covered in oilskins, and a supply of small wooden barrels, linked together in pairs by means of a broad leather strap. McDougal told me that these are called half-ankers, and that each barrel holds a little over four gallons of liquid. They are filled with rum or brandy, and the tubmen carry them from the shore to the tavern where they're hidden away out of sight of the revenue men.

Once all the cargo had been unloaded, I was given one of these half-ankers. Although heavy, it was surprisingly easy to carry: the leather strap sat comfortably on my shoulders and the barrels sat one on my chest and the other on my back. It reminded me a little of the wooden beam which milkmaids use on their shoulders to carry their pails of milk.

John Burgess was given several lengths of coarse rope, which he coiled across his body. This puzzled me at first, as I hadn't thought that rope was something which would need to be smuggled. It was only later that I discovered what the ropes really were: a large and cleverly-disguised quantity of plaited tobacco leaves.

There were also several men I hadn't seen before. They were all tall, thick-set and strong-looking, and would have made light work of carrying the heavy bales or barrels. So I was surprised to see, when we set off back towards the tavern, that they were not carrying any cargo. But it was not long before their true purpose became clear: they positioned themselves around us as we walked, and spent the whole journey looking around over their shoulders. The cudgels they carried betrayed their purpose. These men, it transpired, were called batsmen, and their task was to ensure that we (and the goods we were carrying) should all reach the tavern safely.

My fingers itched to handle one of those cudgels. If I ever had occasion to use one, I would imagine I was using it on Hindley…

But I digress. I came away to try to forget the past.

When we arrived back at The Mermaid, Mistress O'Keefe was waiting for us. One of the batsmen kept watch at an upstairs window and another two stationed themselves just inside the door, whilst the remainder of the gang set about storing away our cargo. As we worked, she prepared a bowl of hot punch to warm us after our long spell out of doors.

As McDougal had said, The Mermaid is full of clever hiding places: inside settles, under floorboards, and behind false panels in the walls. McDougal himself took charge of the half-ankers, which he and I carried upstairs into a secret room hidden behind a wall in one of the attics.

This tiny chamber had no window, and was just long enough for a man to lie full-length, and just high enough to be able to sit up without stooping. Once we had finished stowing away the barrels and were seated by the fire in another space hidden at the back of the tavern, enjoying our tankards of hot punch and some fresh cakes which Mistress O'Keefe had baked for us, McDougal explained to me that the tiny attic room had originally been a priest-hole. It appears that being a Catholic had in the past been fraught with danger, so Catholic families had to go to great measures to conceal their activities – including being able to hide priests in their homes if the King's men came calling. He said that his own mother had once concealed a priest for a whole week.

The man is a constant source of surprise. I wonder what else I have yet to learn about him…

***

William McDougal

Young Heathcliff did a grand job this evening. As he told me during our earlier talk, he's well used to hard work, and this appears to have made him very strong. He certainly made very light work of carrying the half-ankers from the shore back to the tavern, and even when we laboured to stow them away in the old priest-hole, he seemed not to notice their weight.

He seemed genuinely surprised when we went up to the priest-hole (which can only be a good thing – it proves that it's a very good hiding place), but he was even more surprised when I told him why it was there. He seems a bright enough lad, but sadly lacking in education. He can read and write, but his basic general knowledge is very poor. He has no grasp at all of history or geography.

I wonder how he would fare on one of Trelawney's trips. I'll keep him with the land gang for now, but when Trelawney gets back from France I'll ask him how he feels about giving the lad a trial run. Just a short one to start with, I think. Then, depending how he manages with that, we could maybe give him one of the longer trips.

***

Matthew Trelawney

I saw Bill McDougal at the dockside today. He asked me if I might have room for a new recruit on my next run. It seems he's got a new member of his gang – a lad of about seventeen or so, newly arrived from Yorkshire, and desperate for work. Bill's been using him as a tubman for the past couple of weeks, and he's pretty impressed with him. He told me the lad is very strong, quite bright, not afraid of hard work, and – most important – trustworthy.

I told Bill I'd give the lad a try. We're due to do another short trip on the *Ellen May* in a few days, so I'll take him along. I just hope he's up to the job. There's no room for any passengers in our business.

***

35

William McDougal

Tonight, when we got back to The Mermaid after our land run, I took young Heathcliff aside and asked him if he'd like to have a trip out to sea. He looked surprised at the suggestion, and asked what it would involve. It seems that he's never been on a boat before – well, not that he remembers, at any rate.

I told him a little bit about Trelawney and his sea-trips to France, and he seemed very happy to go along with him.

***

Heathcliff

This morning, McDougal took me to the dockside and introduced me to a man named Matthew Trelawney, explaining that he was the captain of a lugger called the *Ellen May*. Not a huge craft, but quite well-equipped, with plenty of space in the hold, and also small but comfortable cabins for the crew.

"Is this your first time out at sea, lad?" Trelawney asked me, as we drew away from the dockside and waved farewell to McDougal.

"Yes," I said. "I must admit I'm not quite sure what to expect."

Trelawney smiled. "Quite an adventure, then?"

I nodded, and took in deep breaths of the fresh salty air. But once the *Ellen May* had left the calm waters of the harbour, the sea became much choppier and I soon began to feel queasy. Trelawney seized my arm and led me to the side of the deck.

"You're looking a bit green, lad," he said. "Watch the horizon. Focus on that, and it will help you to keep your bearings. If you haven't been to sea before it can take a little time to get used to it, but once you've found your sea-legs you'll be fine."

I did as he advised, and it did help to keep the seasickness at bay, but I have no idea how long I stood there. After the *Ellen May* had set off I'd lost all sense of time, save that it was still daylight. I once stole a glance at my pocket-watch, but it had stopped ticking.

I fixed my eyes again on the horizon, and in the distance I could make out the shape of a rugged coastline. "What land is that?" I asked.

"That's Wales," Trelawney explained. "Next, we'll pass Devon and Cornwall, then we'll head across the Channel."

"What? Does that mean we've haven't even left England yet?"

Trelawney chuckled. "Nay, lad, I'm afraid we've still got quite a way to go."

I shuddered. "Where are we going?"

"To France. There is a small port called Roscoff, on the north-west coast. That is where our business is based."

I didn't like to ask exactly what this 'business' might be, though I reasoned it must have some connection with what McDougal was doing back in Liverpool. But judging by the way Trelawney suddenly fell silent, I wondered if he had already said more than he intended.

"How long will our journey take?" I asked – partly in an attempt to steer the conversation back towards calmer, safer waters, but also because I genuinely wanted to know. Before Hindley had stopped my lessons, I'd learned a little about foreign countries, but nothing like enough to grasp any idea of distance.

Trelawney turned back to face me. He looked, and sounded, relieved at the change of subject.

"There and back, about a week, I should think. It's difficult to say exactly, because we're always at the mercy of the wind and the tides. But we're better equipped than some to deal with those."

I was intrigued. "Better equipped in what way?"

Trelawney gestured towards the mast which towered above the deck, and the black sails billowing each side of it. "We're fore-and-aft rigged rather than square-rigged."

This meant nothing to me. He might just as well have been speaking in a foreign language.

"Sorry, but what does that mean?"

Trelawney gave me a look as if to say *Oh Lord, what sort of idiot have I got here?* But he took a deep breath, then addressed me as if speaking to a small and particularly stupid child.

"It means that we can adjust the angle of the sails according to the wind direction. A square-rigged boat – that's one where the sails are set at right angles to the keel – can only move if the wind is directly behind it. Which is fine if the wind is blowing the same way as your boat wants to go, but not so good if you need to sail in the opposite direction. For a business like ours, which relies on secre— er, speed, that's risky. Very risky. We might get into a harbour easily enough, but we'd then be stuck there until the wind changes. We could even get trapped in the harbour if the tide goes out and the wind is in the wrong direction."

"I see. But what's the difference between that and – what did you call it?"

"Fore-and-aft rigging? On a boat, fore means front and aft means back. Look at the way the sails are set. They run along the line of the keel – from the front of the boat to the back. So they don't depend just on wind direction, because we can change the angle of the sails and go slightly up-wind, then turn and head the other way. It's called tacking. It looks a bit odd, but it does work. What's really useful is that we can get in and out of a harbour on the same tide. That's particularly important in our line of work."

I didn't like to admit that I was still confused, but decided that what Trelawney was describing would probably make more sense if I saw it put into practice. For now, though, I just needed to concentrate on focussing on the horizon, keeping upright, and not parting company with the contents of my stomach.

***

Matthew Trelawney

Well, the lad seems keen enough, but I'm amazed at how little he knows. Bill McDougal had warned me that he's very uneducated, but he has no concept at all of geography or distance, and I had to explain the basics of seamanship to him in words of one syllable. I just hope we aren't making a massive mistake with him.

***

Heathcliff

Three days and two nights later, we finally arrived at our destination under cover of darkness. The ship dropped anchor a little way out to sea, and in the distance we could make out the lights of a small town. Trelawney lit a lamp and signalled towards the land, and a few minutes later a small rowing boat set off from the beach and made its way towards us.

As it approached, the two men on board greeted Trelawney like an old friend, but spoke in a strange language which I couldn't understand. Trelawney answered them in what I assumed must be the same tongue, then gestured to me to follow him down into the boat.

"Our cargo is waiting for us ashore," he explained to me, as the rowing boat made its way back towards the shore. "We need to get it on to the ship as quickly as possible, then be on our way as soon as we can."

I remembered what Trelawney had said during the voyage about the need for haste, and I found myself fervently hoping that we would come through this whole exercise without any trouble. Eventually the boat ran aground on a small area of rough pebbles, where we climbed out and scrambled up the beach to dry land.

The two men who had greeted us, who I discovered were called Pierre and Michel, led us to the back of the beach and began to lift piles of brushwood from a mound in the corner. Underneath were stacked a pile of small barrels and tobacco ropes of the type I had previously seen in Liverpool, plus several large bundles wrapped in oilskin. We formed a human chain and gradually transported these items into the rowing boat, though it took four trips out to sea to transport everything on to the ship.

"What is the stuff in the oilskins?" I asked Trelawney, once we had finished and were preparing to set sail.

"Tea," he replied. "It's grown in China and the Far East, and is shipped from there to a port called Lorient, a little further south from here. The port's name means 'East' in French."

"French? Was that the language you were talking just now?"

He nodded. "I've been doing this trip for quite a few years, and in that time I've learned enough to speak to the natives fairly well. I once became quite friendly with a French lady…" His voice trailed off and he stared out to sea.

"How friendly?" I ventured.

"Friendly enough to know that I wanted to marry her," he said, his voice quiet with emotion.

"May I ask why you didn't?" I replied, equally quietly.

"She chose to marry someone else." His voice had an edge which betrayed the pain he obviously still felt. "Someone who could offer her wealth and rank. She clearly valued those things far more than love and honour."

"I know exactly how you feel. That happened to me too."

Trelawney looked up, clearly surprised. "When was this?" he asked.

"A few weeks ago, back in Yorkshire. We've known each other almost all our lives, and I'd always thought she loved me as much as I loved her. I couldn't imagine a future without her, and if I'm honest with myself I still can't. But her brother has always hated me, and the final straw was when I overheard her telling one of the servants – one of the servants, for Heaven's sake! – that it would *degrade* her to marry me."

Trelawney laid a brotherly hand on my arm. "Was that why you came to Liverpool?"

"Yes. I just knew I had to get away. I didn't care where I went, and boarded the first coach I found. That was where it happened to be going."

Trelawney sighed. "Your story sounds very similar to mine. I used to live in Polperro, in Cornwall, and worked as a fisherman. It was hard work for little reward, so I used to supplement my income by helping out with the free traders. I started out doing occasional jobs with the land gangs, then I

40

lost my fishing boat in a storm, so I started working for them full-time. After a little while, because I knew how to handle a boat, they asked me to do some of the runs to the offshore islands – Jersey and Guernsey, mostly – bringing the tea, wine and brandy to England. Then, about fifteen years ago, we had to abandon that route and shift the whole business to France."

"I'm sorry, but what are those islands you mentioned?"

"Jersey and Guernsey? They're quite close to the coast of northern France. Officially, they belong to Britain, but for some reason they have – or rather had – different tax laws, so we could buy stuff there much more cheaply than in Britain. But then the British government put a Customs House on Guernsey and started slapping hefty taxes on goods from there, so that was when we had to move the business to France."

"But I thought we were supposed to be at war with France."

Trelawney grinned. "Officially, yes, we were at the time. But we found an unlikely ally: the King of France. He knew full well that the free trade would be profitable for France – because that was where we were buying the goods – and damaging to Britain because of the loss of tax revenue, so he wasted no time in declaring Roscoff a free port."

It made sense, but I was still surprised. It was plain to see that the money which could be earned from free trade, either in Britain or France, was far more important than allegiance to any kind of authority.

"The change was easy enough to make," Trelawney went on. "Especially for me, because I'd grown up in Cornwall and I knew enough of the Cornish language, which is close enough to the local language they speak in Roscoff, to be able to speak to the locals fairly easily. Learning French came later."

"It all seems a very long way from Liverpool," I remarked. "How did you come to be there?"

"By much the same means as you did, though I came by sea rather than by road. After Louise abandoned me, I jumped on the first boat out of Polperro without a thought about where it was going. It was on its way back to Liverpool. That was where I met Bill McDougal."

"That was where I met him, too. I wonder if he specialises in recruiting waifs and strays!"

Trelawney smiled. "Maybe so. His gang certainly seem to be a curious mixture of people."

As Trelawney said this, I realised I didn't know very much about most of McDougal's gang, but my thoughts returned to the one I'd had most dealings with: John Burgess. He did not seem to me to be particularly 'curious', but the more I thought about it, the more sure I became that there was something about him which I wasn't being told.

***

Matthew Trelawney

I had a long chat with young Heathcliff on the way back from Roscoff. He told me a little about himself and why he'd come to Liverpool. Like me, he was escaping from a woman who broke his heart.

I understand him a lot more now. And he's strong, hard-working, and seems to have good sea-legs. I'll report back to Bill McDougal that I'll be happy to have him on board again.

***

Heathcliff

The journey back was a little quicker than the outward trip, taking two days rather than three, because in this direction the wind was in our favour. It was quite late in the afternoon before we came within sight of Liverpool. Once Trelawney was sure of our position, he sailed the ship a little further out to sea, dropped anchor and waited for nightfall. At his suggestion, I went below decks, grabbed a bite to eat, and managed to sleep for a few hours.

When Trelawney woke me it was dark, save for glimpses of a pale moon through breaks in the cloud. It was only then that I realised why the sails of the *Ellen May* were black: even on a clear moonlit night, the ship would be impossible to spot from the shore. I looked around, but had no notion at all of any

42

sense of direction.

"See, there?" Trelawney said. I followed his pointing finger and could see a very faint light on the horizon. "That's our signal – the coast is clear. The boat is on its way. All hands on deck."

The crew began to bring up the barrels and bundles from the hold. A few minutes later a small rowing boat appeared out of the darkness and drew up alongside the ship, and the cargo was carefully lowered into it. This boat was a little larger than the one in Roscoff, so the transfer of the goods to the shore took only three trips rather than four. On the third trip, Trelawney directed me into the boat, along with the cargo.

"Time for you to go ashore, lad," he said, and patted me on the shoulder before pressing a folded paper into my hand. "Please give this to Bill McDougal. I will see you again, I'm sure."

McDougal was waiting on the beach with some of the other members of the gang. I handed him Trelawney's paper, then busied myself with the task of transporting the cargo back to The Mermaid. As before, it was well past midnight before we had finished and could reward ourselves with our clay pipes and some mugs of hot punch.

McDougal came and sat by me.

"How was your first sea voyage?" he asked, drawing on his pipe.

"Quite unlike anything I've ever known," I answered. "I've always been used to having firm ground under my feet. It took a while to get used to the floor moving."

"Yes, I can well understand that. But Trelawney seemed to think you'd fared very well for a first-timer." He reached into his pocket and pulled out a piece of paper, which I recognised as being the one Trelawney had given me before I'd left the ship, and read aloud:

"Young Heathcliff is a great addition to the crew. Please make sure he is suitably rewarded."

McDougal put the paper down and produced a cloth bag.

"Here is your money. Carry on doing the job as well as you have done so far, and there will be a lot more for you."

I peered inside the bag and looked up in amazement. It was full of silver and gold coins. I knew that McDougal had promised that I would be paid for what I did, yet I had no idea how much. I would have been content to have earned just enough to keep myself fed, and repay Mistress O'Keefe for my board and lodging at The Mermaid. Back at The Heights, after old Mr Earnshaw died, Hindley had forced me to work long hours on the land for nothing – and I'm sure that if he'd had his way, he would have turned me out altogether. He probably only let me stay because Cathy insisted that he must.

Cathy… Oh Cathy, why did you betray me?

I realised McDougal was speaking again.

"…for the remainder of the summer," he said. "Are you happy with that?"

"I'm sorry," I confessed, and held up the bag of coins. "I was so taken aback by this that I missed the start of what you said."

McDougal grinned, and took another draw on his pipe. "I said that Trelawney goes on to say he will be happy to have you join them on the *Ellen May* for the remainder of the summer."

"Thank you," I said. "I am very happy with that." The idea of a summer at sea, taking me away from the heartache of home, was very appealing.

McDougal stood up, patted me on the shoulder, and wandered across to talk to Mistress O'Keefe.

A moment or two later, John Burgess approached me and asked if he might join me. I couldn't help thinking he sounded nervous. I smiled at him, and gestured towards the chair which McDougal had just vacated.

"I thought that venture went fairly well," I said.

"Yes," he answered, opening his tobacco pouch and carefully filling his pipe. "I'm glad McDougal has been prepared to give me another chance."

"Why? What makes you say that?"

He hesitated, then leaned forward before speaking in a low

voice.

"The night you first arrived here, I accidentally dropped this pouch on the floor when the revenue men were around. You covered it with your foot so they didn't see it."

"Yes, I remember. But I thought no more about it afterwards."

"But I did. If the revenue men had spotted it and looked inside, and realised where it had come from, it could have been the ruin of our whole operation." He shuddered.

"Why?" I asked.

He stared at me. "Don't you know the penalties for what we do?"

"I must confess I don't. What are they?"

Burgess looked around, then whispered, "We could all end up on the gallows."

For a moment I was speechless. I genuinely had no idea how closely we were dicing with death.

"But if it's so risky," I asked him, "why do you do it?"

"Because I need the money. My daughter is very sick, and I cannot afford to pay for a doctor on what I earn as a farmer. It's all I can do just to keep body and soul together. If McDougal kicks me out of the gang..." His voice trailed off and he stared at the floor.

During the silence which followed, I thought back to what had happened back at The Heights the night I left. A little while before I heard Cathy say it would degrade her to marry me, Hindley (in the throes of drunken idiocy) had held his young son Hareton over the bannisters on the first floor and let him fall. I was standing right underneath, and by instinct I caught the boy before he hit the ground.

Immediately afterwards, I realised how Hindley would have felt if Hareton had died. At the time I was angry with myself because I'd missed the opportunity of getting some kind of revenge on Hindley. But seeing how concerned John Burgess was for his sick child, and how devastated he would be if he lost her, I now had some idea how a father must feel.

"Have you told Mr McDougal about this?" I whispered.

Burgess glanced across towards the bar, where McDougal

was standing talking to Mistress O'Keefe. Once satisfied that we wouldn't be overheard, he leaned towards me before answering.

"I haven't dared. I know how he feels about 'carrying passengers', as he'd describe it. I'm sailing very close to the wind as it is. If he wants an excuse to get rid of me, this would be a gift on a silver tray."

I reached into the bag McDougal had given me, and pulled out one of the gold coins.

"Here," I said. "Take this and buy your daughter some medicine, or pay for a doctor to see her."

He looked up at me, open-mouthed and seemingly lost for words.

"Go on," I repeated. "I don't know how much it will buy, but—"

"What?" he gasped, having found his voice at last. "This will buy far more than I could ever dream of affording. Thank you so much. How can I ever repay you?"

"By using it to help make her well again. Knowing that it's done some good would be repayment enough."

Looking at his face, and seeing sadness and fear replaced by joy and hope, I found myself wondering if I'll ever be a father myself. I very much doubt it, unless Cathy ever changes her mind about marrying Edgar Linton. I certainly can't imagine ever having a child with anyone else.

***

John Burgess

Young Heathcliff has proved to be my saviour yet again. When I told him about little Emily, he gave me a sovereign from his own earnings so that I could pay for treatment for her.

But for all his good qualities, he seems like a troubled soul. I can see it in his eyes. I'd love to know what he's running away from.

***

Autumn 1780

Heathcliff

I've worked with Trelawney for most of the summer, during which time I learned much of the life of a sailor. As well as 'fore' and 'aft', I soon discovered other terms which land-based folk wouldn't understand: 'bow' and 'stern' for the front and rear of the vessel, and 'larboard' and 'starboard' for the left- and right-hand sides. Trelawney explained that these last two meant 'loading side' and 'steering side'. It made some kind of sense, I suppose.

The regular runs between Liverpool and Roscoff, ferrying wine and brandy from France and tea from the Far East, netted us a healthy profit over the course of those summer months. McDougal even accompanied us on one or two of the voyages, and was thrilled to discover that Roscoff had been the place from whence the young Queen Mary Stuart had set sail when she had left France to return to her native Scotland. He explained to me that she was a direct ancestor of Bonnie Prince Charlie – the one he'd called 'the King over the Water'. McDougal is adamant that Prince Charlie's claim to the English throne is far stronger than that of King George.

I don't fully understand it, but I'm sure he knows what he's talking about.

***

Matthew Trelawney

It was interesting taking Bill McDougal along to France with us. He's always seemed obsessed with this 'King over the Water' business, but he was utterly delighted when he found out about the link with Roscoff and Mary Queen of Scots.

"Just think," he said, "I'm treading the same ground that she trod!"

To be honest, I don't think I've seen him look so animated for quite a long time.

***

It's two days since Trelawney and I returned from our latest trip on the *Ellen May*. This afternoon, McDougal joined me in the bar of The Mermaid and presented me with a brimming tankard.

"I've been keeping an eye on you, young Heathcliff," he said, "and I've been very pleased with what I've seen. Now that you've shown me what you're made of, I think you're ready for greater things. How do you feel about taking a longer voyage, with the chance of much bigger profits?"

This sounded very attractive. "What would it involve?" I asked. "Please tell me more."

"I won't deny that it's difficult, and often dangerous. But for those who have the stomach for it, it's the most profitable trade in the world." He paused, and gestured towards our surroundings. "How do you think The Mermaid is funded?"

I was puzzled. "I thought it came from free trade."

McDougal shrugged. "Well, it does up to a point, but that's just the tip of the iceberg. Mistress O'Keefe runs an efficient tavern here, and she does a grand job in looking after us and keeping the revenue men off our trail…"

"She's an excellent cook, too," I added, with a grin.

McDougal nodded, and returned my smile. "That she is. She's been running The Mermaid for me for more than ten years now. I came across her when she was seriously down on her luck and desperate to change her life, and I recognised that she'd be the ideal person for the task." His face grew serious, and he looked around to check that the lady herself was out of earshot before continuing. "She never talks about her early life, and nobody ever asks her about it. She originally came from Ireland – that much she does admit to – but that's as much as anyone here knows."

"I see. Thank you."

"But the tavern itself… Well, let's just say it owes its main livelihood to another source of income – about which the less is known, the better."

By now I was intrigued. "What do you mean?"

McDougal leaned forward and beckoned me closer to him. "It's called the Triangular Trade. The boat makes a three-stage journey. You and Trelawney will set off from here with a cargo of goods exported from England – iron and copper bars, muskets, gunpowder, beads, looking-glasses – and sail to the coast of West Africa where you'll trade those goods for your next cargo, about which more in a moment. Then you'll transport that cargo across the Atlantic; sometimes to the West Indies, at other times to the Americas, where you'll trade it for goods to bring back to England: cotton, tobacco, wood, sugar and rum. I must warn you that the middle passage will be the most challenging, but you'll earn a share of the profits of each voyage, and in a very short time you'll be a very rich man."

I could be rich? It was purely because I was poor that Cathy had said she wouldn't marry me. If I could be rich, then maybe, after all, I might be able win her back…

"Why are you telling me all this?" I whispered.

"Because, young Heathcliff, I sense in you a kindred spirit. You are not afraid of hard work, you've proved to me that you can be trusted, and you don't suffer fools – or foolish rules – gladly. I've been childless all my life, but in some ways you seem like the son I never had."

I was touched at his words. "I never knew my parents," I told him. "I was a foundling, brought up by a kindly man who took me in and treated me as though I were his own. But since I've been here you've taken me under your wing in a way I'd never imagined. I'd be happy to think of you as an honorary father."

I looked up at him and caught him smiling at me.

"Thank you," he said quietly.

"But what about that second stage of cargo?" I asked. "What does that involve?"

McDougal's face grew serious, and he lowered his voice so that I could barely make out his words. "It's a trade in human flesh," he murmured.

I gasped. "You mean…?"

McDougal nodded. "Yes. Slaves."

***

William McDougal

Well, it's done. I've invited young Heathcliff to join Trelawney on the Triangular Route.

I know he's a hard-working and trustworthy soul, but he also seems to have a sensitive side which he keeps well hidden. But then, it was the same with Trelawney when he first started. I'll have a quiet word with him beforehand and see if he can prepare the lad for the middle passage.

***

Heathcliff

This time, when I met Matthew Trelawney at the dockside, he was not captaining the *Ellen May*. Instead, he led me aboard a much bigger brig called the *Mersey Rose*.

The dockhands were already hard at work, carrying crates of cargo aboard the brig and storing them in the hold. Trelawney introduced me to the rest of the crew (a cook, a doctor, and half a dozen deck-hands) then showed me to my quarters: a narrow cabin with a small table and chair, and a bunk just wide enough for me to lie flat on my back. Below the bunk was a sea-chest for my few possessions. Trelawney's own cabin, identical in style but slightly bigger in size, was adjacent to my own.

"Not exactly the last word in comfort," he said, with a stoical shrug of his broad shoulders, "but I expect we'll survive."

"Where exactly are we going?"

"First, we'll call in the port of Lisbon, to collect provisions, and from there sail to the island of Madeira. After that, we'll make our way to the west coast of Africa, where we'll trade our goods on board for the next lot of cargo, which we transport westwards to the Caribbean. Then we exchange that cargo for a further consignment to bring back to England. Rum and sugar, mostly."

"How long will it take, do you think?"

"That depends. Sometimes we reach Africa in a little over two months; at other times it can take nearly four. But for now, just enjoy the voyage."

***

Matthew Trelawney

I know young Heathcliff is strong, and I don't think he shocks easily, but I think he might be in for a nasty surprise when we get to Africa. I'm not sure whether I should try to prepare him more fully for what's in store, or whether to let him carry on for the moment in blissful ignorance. Bill McDougal told me that he'd explained the procedure to Heathcliff in general terms, but recalling my own first experience of the Triangular Trade, I wish I'd been warned beforehand about the middle passage. When we arrived at the Congo it was definitely a baptism of fire.

Perhaps I'd better tell him a bit more. Forewarned, as they say, is forearmed.

***

Heathcliff

It must be way past midnight now, but I can't sleep. My mind is throbbing with what Trelawney told me this evening.

We'd set sail from Liverpool on the evening tide, and crossed the Irish Sea to Cork to take on more supplies for the voyage. It was very stormy, and we were forced to drop anchor in Cork harbour and wait for the weather to improve.

After dinner, Trelawney and I sat in his cabin with our clay pipes, and he explained a little more about what our so-called 'triangular trip' would involve. True, McDougal had told me that the middle passage would be the most challenging, but he hadn't gone into any detail, so I was totally unprepared for what I was about to hear.

Trelawney unrolled the charts and described the route we would take.

"This is where we are now, on the southern coast of Ireland.

51

This country here is France, and this," (he pointed to an area of land jutting out from the north-west coast) "is Cape Finisterre. In French that means 'the end of the world', and it might have seemed like it on our trips to Roscoff, but believe me, we'll be travelling a lot further than that this time."

I watched as he named and explained the various places we would pass. "This is the Bay of Biscay, and here, lying to the south of France, are the countries of Spain and Portugal. When we reach Portugal, we will call in the port of Lisbon, here, to take on more supplies, then sail on to Madeira."

"Where is that?"

Trelawney pointed to a large landmass lying to the south of the country he'd called Spain. "This," he said, "is the continent of Africa. This island here, to the west, is Madeira (which belongs to Portugal). We will call in there for more supplies before heading for our main destination, here." His finger traced the line of a large curve on the western edge of Africa. "The official maps will call this the Ivory Coast, or the Gold Coast. But in truth, this whole area, around three thousand miles from the Cape Verde islands – here – to the mouth of the Congo River – here – is the Slave Coast."

I gasped. "So – what happens when we get there?"

Trelawney leaned back on his chair and took a long draught on his pipe, then blew smoke-rings into the air above our heads.

"That," he said, with an unfamiliar hardness in his voice which chilled me to the bone, "is where the real dealings take place. We trade our English goods with the local dealers, negotiate the purchases of the slaves, then transport them across the Atlantic to the West Indies." He leaned forward again and traced the route on the chart as he spoke. "There, we sell them for the best price we can get. Afterwards, we collect our cargo of rum and sugar from Barbados – here – then back across the Atlantic to Liverpool. That's what we'll be doing this time. Other times, we go to the east coast of America – here – to trade the slaves for cotton and tobacco, but we aren't doing that on this trip."

I said nothing as I took in the meaning of his words. "How

long have you been doing this?" I asked eventually, for want of something to break the uncomfortable silence.

"This is my third year," he answered, without emotion.

"And does it not shock you?"

He hesitated before answering. "It did at first," he said. "On my first trip I found it hard to believe that men could treat their fellow-men – and women – so brutally. But," he shrugged, "I soon realised that it is their way of life, and there is no point in fighting it. The African natives are savages who would happily trade their own grandmothers for a handful of trinkets."

"You mean...?"

"Yes. It is not just the white traders who deal in black flesh. Their own chieftains are just as greedy. We give them what they want, and they give us the means of making a not-so-small fortune. There is always a heavy demand for slaves to work the plantations in the West Indies and America, and a good crop of strong men can command a high price. Everyone wins. Except the slaves, of course," he added with a sneer.

I was silent as I took in Trelawney's words. Truth to tell, I was horrified – not just at his words, but also at his change of demeanour. I thought back to the first voyage I'd made with him, and especially our conversation about betrayal and lost love. I wondered if Trelawney's hardness of heart might have anything to do with his own heart having been broken so brutally, just as my own had been.

In which case, could I also be destined for a lifetime bereft of humanity and compassion? Only time will tell...

***

Matthew Trelawney

I told him, as simply as I could, what was involved. Not surprisingly, he appeared shocked, just as I had been when I made my first trip with Bill McDougal. I can see that he will need to cultivate a hardness of heart if he's going to get through this. But there's no turning back now.

***

After the storm had died down, we were able to weigh anchor and begin our long journey southwards. The passage which Trelawney had called the Bay of Biscay was consistently rough, and we found ourselves obliged to stay within sight of land for the whole time in order to minimise the discomfort. I was concerned that we might be apprehended by other, more official, craft, but Trelawney reassured me that even in the unlikely event of this happening, we would be quite safe. We were carrying nothing illegal. In this respect, at least, we were far more law-abiding than we had been on any of our trips from Roscoff.

The city of Lisbon was a welcome sight: a hillside of pretty white houses topped with roofs of orange tiles, and at the summit a huge cathedral and an imposing-looking castle. As we docked, the air felt fresh and warm – a pleasant relief from the cold northern winds we had left behind. Our provisions were replenished with crates of fresh fruit and vegetables, a few barrels of Portuguese wine, and several bundles of dried salted codfish. The latter gave off an unfamiliar but sharp aroma which stuck in my throat.

"You'll be heartily sick of this by the time we reach Africa," Trelawney warned me, as we loaded the pungent bundles into the hold. "But we take it on board because it's one of the few foodstuffs which doesn't rot in transit. The Portuguese seem to love it, though goodness only knows why. As far as I'm concerned, it's the piece of cod which passeth all understanding."

I chuckled.

"It's claimed that the Portuguese have a different way of preparing it for every day of the year," Trelawney went on. "Be that as it may, I only wish our cook could find just one way of making it appetising."

"It looks barely edible," I remarked. "Why is it so dry and flat?"

"It's preserved in barrels of salt," Trelawney explained, "and it has to be soaked in water for hours before it can be

54

eaten. But our cook tends to skimp on the soaking, so the end result is usually very chewy, and always tastes saltier than it should." He grimaced, then smiled and patted one of the barrels of wine. "But this stuff more than makes up for it, believe me. And just wait until we get to Madeira. They have some of the finest wines on earth."

***

Matthew Trelawney

It felt good to be back in Lisbon. The town is always so welcoming, and the food and wine are delicious. Apart from that confounded codfish, of course. Poor Heathcliff doesn't know what's coming to him.

***

Heathcliff

My first taste of the codfish came shortly after we left Lisbon. As Trelawney had predicted, it was tough and dry, and any flavour it might have had was murdered by its overwhelming saltiness.

"I'd love to know how the Portuguese cook this," I muttered, chewing hard and taking regular sips of wine to keep my mouth moist.

"A lot better than what we've got here, I'm sure," Trelawney grunted. "They're discerning folk. I know they'd never put up with it like this." Eventually, he pushed his plate aside and reached for the bowl of fruit. "Did you know," he remarked, as he began to peel an apple, "that it's the Portuguese we have to thank for the English love of tea?"

I looked up in surprise and shook my head. "To be honest, it had never occurred to me to wonder about it. But why?"

"One of our kings married a Portuguese princess, and she was the one who introduced tea to England. But it became so popular that the government soon realised it could earn them a handsome profit. Hence the massive tax on it – and hence the free trade." He grinned. "We have many reasons to be thankful

55

to our Portuguese friends. Including the main reason for this voyage."

I choked on my wine. "What? You mean…?"

"Yes. Our contact on the Slave Coast is a Portuguese businessman."

"Another friend of McDougal?"

Trelawney grinned. "Who else?"

"McDougal certainly seems to be very well-connected," I remarked.

"I'd swear he has more pies than fingers to put in them. I've long since given up wondering how he knows all these people. On the whole, I think it's probably better that we don't know."

"Least said, soonest mended?"

Trelawney drained his wine. "Something like that."

***

Matthew Trelawney

Well, as I predicted, the codfish was not particularly well received. Heathcliff made a valiant attempt to force it down, but I could tell he wasn't enjoying it.

What he doesn't know is that we have tons of the stuff, which has to last us until we get to Barbados – and that includes the daily rations for the slaves. What he also doesn't yet know is that it will be his job to dole it out to them. It will stink out the slave decks, but I suppose it's marginally better than what they usually end up stinking of. I don't feel capable of telling him about that in advance, though. Anticipation can only make it worse.

He was much more appreciative of the wine, though.

***

Heathcliff

Our next port of call was the island of Madeira. From a distance, it appeared to be nothing more than a large rock in the middle of the ocean, but as we approached it became apparent that the island was covered in lush vegetation.

56

Trelawney explained that this is what gave the island its name (in Portuguese, the word *madeira* means wood), and that it owes its impressive height to the fact that it was originally a volcano.

The island's main product is its particular brand of wine. Once we had docked in Funchal harbour, we took delivery of twelve barrels, along with a further supply of fresh fruit, local sweetmeats, and – joy of joys – fresh fish. We knew that this would need to be eaten quickly before it turned rancid, but it made a welcome change from the everlasting salt-dried cod.

The wine was, as Trelawney had promised, particularly fine, with a distinctive sweet flavour. This comes from a strong spirit which is added to the wine to preserve it from the heat. I thought back to Hindley and his fondness for strong drink purely for its own sake, and could not imagine him appreciating anything as good as this. The brute might have stopped my lessons back at The Heights, but I was learning far more on this voyage than he would ever know.

Once again, my thoughts turned to Cathy. How I would dearly love to show her all these new wonders…

As we sailed further south the weather steadily grew hotter. We always stayed within sight of the African coast, but the land was visible only through a thick, shimmering haze. By day, the sky was blue and cloudless; by night, it was inky black and peppered with thousands of stars. To me, of course, all this was totally uncharted territory. But Trelawney, who knew the area well from previous voyages, was happy to keep me up to date with our progress.

"We'll soon be approaching the equator," he told me one day, pointing out the line on the map. (I was relieved that he did this, as it saved my displaying even more of my ignorance by having to ask what he meant.)

"How can you tell?" I asked.

"Look at your shadow. Have you noticed that as we've been travelling, your shadow has been getting shorter? At the equator, the sun is directly overhead, and you'll cast hardly any shadow at all. It will just look like a little pool around your feet."

This was a far cry from the cold Yorkshire moors, I thought, as I shielded my eyes from the sweltering sunlight. And we had not even completed the first stage of our trip. What else, I wondered, might be lying in store?

A few days later, I noticed a subtle change in the landscape. The shimmering haze which until now had shrouded the coast by day had suddenly grown thick and smoky, and by night the shoreline was lit by a long line of blazing bonfires.

"See that?" Trelawney pointed, as we slowly approached the land. "That's the signal that they have slaves for sale."

"But why are there so many?" I asked.

Trelawney shrugged. "Do you remember what I said about the Slave Coast? It runs for hundreds of miles, and every village and every tribe is part of it. As soon as they see our sails, they light the bonfires to attract our attention."

"What?"

"Yes. As I said, they are all at it. In truth, they've been at it for centuries. Any chief will sell any member of his village, or even any member of his own family, if they are of no further use to him."

I was dumbstruck.

***

Matthew Trelawney

Poor lad. He still has no idea what's really in store...

***

Heathcliff

We dropped anchor at a place called Lagos, on the coast of the Gulf of Guinea. Making our way ashore, we were met by McDougal's contact, a lavishly-dressed gentleman with skin the colour of pale ale. He greeted Trelawney as one would a long-lost friend.

"Ah, Senhor Trelawney! It is good to see you again!"

"You too, Senhor da Costa. May I present my colleague, Mr Heathcliff."

We shook hands. His handshake was firm and strong.

"I have plenty for you this time, Senhor Trelawney. But first, please join me for refreshments."

We followed him through the steamy dense undergrowth. By the time we arrived at his house, we were all drenched with sweat and covered with small weals from the swarms of biting insects. But the interior was pleasantly cool, aired by palm-leaf fans swinging from the ceiling and operated by a team of silent and morose-looking men. They were clad only in the briefest of loin-cloths, and their skin was the same colour as Cathy's dark brown eyes.

This was the first time I'd seen anyone with a dark skin. Until this voyage, I'd had no idea that such people even existed.

Senhor da Costa motioned us to be seated, then clicked his fingers and said something in a language I didn't understand. A few moments later another dark-skinned man appeared, bearing a tray of glasses. These contained what proved to be a delicious cooling brew, which Trelawney told me was made with lemons grown on the land nearby.

"And now, to business! How many do you require this time, Senhor Trelawney?"

"We have space for around four hundred and fifty."

Senhor da Costa considered for a moment. "If you can take five hundred, I can give you a very good deal."

I caught my breath. *Five hundred?* Where in Heaven's name were we going to accommodate five hundred people?

Trelawney appeared not to have noticed my reaction – or if he had, he chose to take no heed of it. "I will see what we can arrange," he said carefully.

Senhor da Costa beamed and clapped his hands. "Excellent! We shall go and look at the goods in the morning. In the meantime, would you care to join me for dinner this evening?"

"Thank you, we should be delighted. Until later, then."

"Of course we can take five hundred," Trelawney whispered to me, as soon as we were out of range of Senhor da Costa's hearing. "I knew that all along. But in dealings of this kind you must always leave room for negotiation."

"But where are we going to put them? The ship only has quarters for the crew!"

"Quarters?" Trelawney guffawed. "What on earth makes you think they have their own quarters? They are cargo, and they travel as cargo."

***

Matthew Trelawney

Oh dear God in Heaven. I had no idea how little the lad knows. I can only assume that Bill McDougal must have spared him the worst of the details when he recruited him.

I can see that I'll have to teach him to harden his heart, just as I had to learn to do. Otherwise, he's going to be neither use nor ornament.

***

Heathcliff

This morning, Senhor da Costa took us to the slave compound.

The area was packed with men, women and children. The women and children were herded into cages, but the men were shackled together in long iron chains, each man's neck locked into a heavy iron ring. All of them were as dark-skinned as Senhor da Costa's house-slaves, and all were wearing next to nothing. I had never seen women without clothes before, and, truth to tell, I found the sight quite unnerving.

Trelawney, evidently sensing my unease, whispered to me that this was quite normal for the African people. And indeed, they did not appear to be embarrassed at their nakedness – except when the overseers began closely inspecting those body parts which are usually kept hidden from view.

"Why are they doing that?" I whispered.

"They're checking that they're clean," Trelawney whispered back.

"Clean?"

"No traces of the pox."

"What? But why would they need to check for that?"

"The customers don't want to buy damaged goods. The pox can make the men unfit to work, and the women a danger to their masters."

"Danger? What sort of danger?"

Trelawney gasped. "Good God, Heathcliff, do you know nothing?"

My eyes widened as the awful truth struck me. "So – the women are…?" The rest of the question stuck in my throat.

"Yes. The more comely ones, at least. And possibly the less comely ones as well, if their masters are desperate."

The idea of women being no more than the property of men was not new to me (it was the same back in England), but somehow this seemed far more disturbing. Thankfully, I was spared the need to think of a suitable reply, because at that point the overseer called out to attract our attention.

"Well, gentlemen? Are you happy with what you see?"

'Happy' was certainly not the word I would have chosen. But Trelawney simply nodded, and turned to converse with Senhor da Costa. They spoke in low tones and I couldn't make out what they were saying, but judging by the fact that they eventually smiled and shook hands, I presumed that they had negotiated a deal which suited both of them.

Whatever that might be, I decided I didn't want to know the details. It was less than four and twenty hours since our arrival in Africa, but what I had learned during that time was already more than enough to last me for at least half a lifetime.

***

Matthew Trelawney

Heathcliff did not want to take part in the negotiations with Senhor da Costa, and I didn't see any point in insisting that he should – at least not at this stage. He'll have to toughen up a lot if he's going to do this again, but for now he still appears to be in a state of shock. But I was staggered to see how naïf he is with regard to what will happen to the women. He must have led a really sheltered life back in Yorkshire.

61

By letting Senhor da Costa believe that he had sold me fifty more slaves than I had originally wanted, the deal was struck without any difficulty. We would take three hundred and fifty adult males, seventeen boys, and one hundred and thirty-three women and girls, at one pound and ten shillings each. That price leaves plenty of scope for a good profit when we get to Barbados.

***

Heathcliff

The scene at the slave compound was disturbing enough, but much worse was to follow.

Once the deal had been struck, the *Mersey Rose* was 'prepared' to accommodate her new 'cargo'. As soon as the trade goods we had brought from England had been unloaded from the middle deck, this was cleared and fitted with shackles and lengths of chain. This, I learned, was where the adult males would spend the next stage of the voyage. The women and children, meanwhile, would be confined to a wooden cage at one end, with a floor area of just sixteen feet by eighteen feet.

Within hours, the human chain of slaves was brought to the ship by the overseer and a group of henchmen. The slaves shuffled, weeping and wailing, along the quayside, along the gangplank and into what would become their floating prison. Some risked a final glance backwards at their homeland, earning themselves the sharp end of a henchman's whip. I turned away, unable to watch, and at that point I caught sight of the paper in Trelawney's hand:

Three hundred and fifty adult males, seventeen boys, one hundred and thirty-three women and girls, supplied from the Asante, Igbo, Fanti and Yoruba tribes. Price agreed: One pound and ten shillings each.

One pound and ten shillings each. Not humans, just commodities for sale.

We set sail on the evening tide and headed westwards. Soon, we reached the open sea, but the sound of the waves could not cover the constant wailing from below decks. And it was not long before even the fresh air above decks was tainted by a foul and putrid stench seeping up from the hold – a stomach-turning cocktail of sweat, shit and fear.

"Will they stay there for the whole of the passage?" I asked Trelawney. I was afraid of what he would say, but nonetheless I had to know.

"Not all the time," he replied. "They need to be kept fit, so they'll be brought up on to the deck for exercise. But only a few at a time, and they need to be kept in chains. Otherwise, they'll try to escape."

"Escape? How? Where would they go?"

He stared at me. "Where else? Over the side."

"But wouldn't they drown?"

"Of course." His matter-of-fact tone made my blood run cold. "That's why they have to be kept chained together. That way, if one of them makes a run for it, he can't escape without dragging all the others down with him. But some of them are so desperate that they'd rather die on the journey than face what's in store for them at the end of it." He shrugged. "Some of them may well die anyway. But we need to make sure that disease and death are kept to a minimum. That's why we have a doctor on board. Dead or rotting meat is of no value to us."

Once again, I found myself lost for words.

I stared out to sea and watched the setting sun. The sky turned first to orange, then to purple, then to dark blue, then to star-studded inky black – all in the space of less than half an hour. The spectacle was breathtaking, and could hardly be more different from the horrors of what was happening only a few feet below where I was standing.

Trading in goods was one thing. My conscience had scarcely troubled me about that – and there was a certain satisfaction to be gained from helping ordinary people at the expense of authority which wasn't worthy of the title. But trading in human beings? This was something else entirely.

But Trelawney had obviously hardened his heart to what we

were doing. If I was going to stand any chance at all of surviving this ghastly venture, then I must learn to do the same.

***

Matthew Trelawney

Well, we're on our way at last, and it's time for me to adopt the persona of the hardened trader. I just hope Heathcliff doesn't take it all the wrong way. I've grown very fond of the lad, and I'd hate to think it could sour our friendship.

***

Heathcliff

This morning, Trelawney handed me another piece of paper.

"This is their daily ration," he said. "Your task is to take charge of handing it out. No more, no less."

The list made grim reading:

Per adult per day: six ounces of bread, a pound and a half of beans, eight ounces of yams, three ounces of dried fish, twelve pints of water.

The slaves' rations were stored, along with our own, in the lower hold. To reach it, I had to pass through the stinking, wailing slave decks. I held my breath and covered my ears to blot out the stench and the sound. *Harden your heart*, I repeated to myself, over and over again. If I said it often enough, it might eventually come to pass.

Harden your heart... I recited those words many times over the course of the next forty-nine days.

My daylight hours were filled with doling out the daily rations and taking my turn at supervising the exercise (it was known on board as 'dancing on deck', though there was no joy in it for anyone involved). The bread grew gradually more and more stale and the water more and more stagnant, yet these poor creatures in my charge seized it from my hands and gulped it down as though it were a king's banquet. I could just about cope with these degrading tasks if I could avoid looking the slaves in the eye. That way, I could also avoid thinking of them as human beings.

My evenings were eased by generous measures of grog and tobacco, whilst my nights were lonely, long and dreamless. Once or twice, when I found myself unable to sleep, I took a walk on deck, and came across some of the crew manhandling the women and forcing themselves on them. Some of the women were screaming, others were weeping quietly – but their assailants clearly had no regard for their feelings or welfare. The sailors seemed to treat the whole matter as some kind of violent sport.

Finally, after six weeks which passed like six years, we sighted our destination: the island of Barbados. I knew from looking at Trelawney's charts that we would drop anchor in Carlisle Bay, just offshore from Bridgetown. Within half an hour of our arrival, a small boat was making its way towards us from the harbour. It settled alongside the *Mersey Rose*, and a small man made his way nimbly up the ladder and on to the deck. Like Senhor da Costa, he greeted Trelawney like an old friend. Trelawney introduced him as Senhor José Sorges – another Portuguese business associate of the very well-connected William McDougal.

Senhor Sorges had a broad smile and a genial manner. He bade us welcome to Barbados and invited us to join him that evening for dinner, which Trelawney readily accepted. Senhor Sorges promised to send his boat to collect us at five in the afternoon, then shook hands with us and took his leave.

Trelawney gestured towards the island. "What do you think?" he asked, with far more animation and feeling than I had seen in him since before we left Africa.

"It looks wonderful. And after that voyage, the prospect of getting off this ship is very appealing."

Trelawney grinned. "It is indeed. But on the whole, I think we've fared quite well on this trip."

"In what way?"

"It's usually a lot worse. Last time, for example, we lost nearly fifty men to the bloody flux, and three of the women died in childbirth. But we've had nothing like that this time, thank goodness. Even the weather has been kind to us."

"What happens now?"

"We'll spend a few days here. The slaves will be taken off and sold, then the ship will be thoroughly cleaned and dried, and re-loaded ready for the journey home."

I said nothing, but my face must have betrayed my concern, because Trelawney quickly added, "Don't worry. Our friend Senhor Sorges will take care of all that, whilst we have a well-earned rest."

***

Matthew Trelawney

It feels good to be back in Barbados. A paradise island indeed – for those who have the means to appreciate it, of course. For others... Well, the less thought about that, the better.

Only a few more days to go, then I can shed this mask and begin to act like a human being once again. But first, there remains the small matter of the sale. Heathcliff appears to have managed quite well with the middle passage on the whole, but it still remains to be seen how he will cope with the slave market.

***

Heathcliff

A few hours later, we were seated on the terrace of a beautiful house overlooking Bridgetown, eating one of the finest meals I have ever tasted. A delicious vegetable potage, honey-glazed roast ham garnished with herbs, and sweet fresh fruit of a type I had never previously encountered, but which tasted as though we were eating sunshine itself. The food was washed down with local wine and followed by the finest Havana cigars and rum punch. After so long spent at sea and so many weeks of monotonous fare, this truly felt like Heaven on earth.

I was shocked to think how easily, and how quickly, we had forgotten the misery of the voyage.

We stayed in Bridgetown, as guests of Senhor Sorges, for around a week. During that time the *Mersey Rose* was cleaned inside and out by our host's own army of slaves. The process, he explained, was called 'careening'. It was a complicated procedure which I didn't fully understand, but it appeared to involve emptying the ship of all its contents, scrubbing it out, flooding the hold (half at a time) and allowing the tide to wash away the filth, then leaving the ship to dry out in the sunshine. I must confess I felt uneasy about the process (though the prospect of being stranded here in Barbados was not without its attractions), but Trelawney assured me that it was quick and efficient.

And so it proved. By the time the first batch of slaves was brought to auction three days later, the *Mersey Rose* was gleaming inside and out, as though she had only just emerged from the boatyard. The slaves, too, appeared in a rather better state than I had seen them on the ship. I wondered if this was due to better conditions on land than those they had endured on board, and remarked on this to Trelawney, but he replied with a shrug that this was more likely because they had been washed and shaved, and their skins rubbed with oil. This, he added, would disguise any skin blemishes and make them look healthier, and thus increase their sale price.

The men were no longer chained together as they had been in Africa and during the voyage, but each man now wore a thick ankle chain, around four feet in length, at the end of which was a heavy iron ball. The men carried these weights in their hands as they shuffled along, and laid them on the ground when they stood still. In either case, any hopes of escape from this human cattle-market were instantly dashed.

The men and women all now wore simple cotton aprons which covered them from their waists to halfway down their thighs. This attire was more modest than what they had worn (or rather not worn) previously, but still left very little to the imagination. The customers – of which there were many – could all see exactly what they were buying. As the auctioneer mounted the stand and prepared to begin the sale, I thought of the nocturnal activities I had witnessed during the voyage, and recalled what Trelawney had said about what would probably happen to the women once they had been sold. In spite of the morning's heat, I shivered.

My thoughts, as if of their own accord, once again returned to Cathy. Then it struck me like a thunderbolt: just like these poor women standing under the sweltering sun and awaiting their fate, she too was being sold and would become a man's property. The only difference was that in the case of her and Edgar Linton, she was the one who was doing the selling.

***

Matthew Trelawney

Heathcliff seemed to cope reasonably well with the auction, but at one point he shielded his eyes (as if from the sun) and turned away. When he looked up again he appeared to have a trace of a tear on his cheek.

I wonder what was going through his mind?

***

Heathcliff

The auction was finished by midday, and Senhor Sorges declared himself well satisfied with the outcome. The profit, it transpired, ran not into hundreds of pounds, but thousands. With a second similar sale to come the following day, there was every prospect that this figure would double.

My head was reeling. The sum was so large that I could not even begin to envisage it – although, for the first time, I began to understand the attraction which this degrading trade might hold for McDougal, Trelawney, and anyone else who takes part in it…

***

Matthew Trelawney

The profit far exceeded any sum we have achieved in the past. Ten thousand five hundred pounds on the first day, and twelve thousand two hundred pounds on the second.

Bill McDougal will be mightily pleased.

***

Heathcliff

When we left Bridgetown four days later, the *Mersey Rose* betrayed no clue about her previous cargo. The hold was now filled with fresh food for our homeward journey, together with barrels of blended rum and crates full of sugar cones, plus some boxes of the original cargo from our outward journey. These, Trelawney explained, had not been needed for trade in Africa, so would be taken home ready to be used on the next voyage. It also transpired that he and Senhor da Costa had negotiated the purchase of several cases of ivory, which would command a good price amongst the dealers back in Liverpool.

During the voyage back to England, Trelawney and I regained the camaraderie which we had enjoyed on the outward journey to Africa. During the middle passage he had been cold and aloof, but I now decided that he must have erected an invisible barrier around himself in order to survive the ordeal – as indeed I had forced myself to do. But now all that was behind us, and our cargo gave us no trouble. The prospect of the riches awaiting us on our return was enough to sweeten the rough passage across the Atlantic.

***

Summer 1781

Heathcliff

Finally, after fifty-five days at sea, we sailed gratefully into Liverpool harbour. McDougal, who must have been forewarned of our return, was on the quayside to greet us.

"Welcome home, gentlemen! A good voyage?"

"Very successful, thank you," Trelawney replied. "I think you will be well pleased with the outcome."

McDougal climbed on board and scrambled down into the hold. He spent a little time inspecting the cargo, then checked the paperwork and declared himself satisfied.

"Excellent work, gentlemen. Shall we adjourn to The Mermaid for a celebratory drink and discuss your remuneration?"

Trelawney and I both nodded agreement. Stepping off the *Mersey Rose* on to dry land felt like a true homecoming, and my mouth watered at the prospect of once again sampling some of Mistress O'Keefe's finest cooking.

But as we pushed open the door of The Mermaid, we sensed immediately that something was wrong. Mistress O'Keefe rushed to meet us, her face livid with fear.

"Mr McDougal, have you heard? Mr Burgess has been arrested."

***

Matthew Trelawney

John Burgess has been arrested? Oh good Heavens.

I must confess I haven't had very much to do with John Burgess. Bill McDougal has told me in the past that he's no sailor, so my only contact with him has been occasional meetings at The Mermaid. I did once hear a rumour that in the past he had a very close shave with the press gang, and ended up having to hide in the priest-hole. I've no idea if that's true or not, but it would certainly explain why he shies away from going to sea.

But now, we all need to band together. I'm sure Bill McDougal will have a plan.

***

Heathcliff

"Arrested?" McDougal gasped. "What happened?"

"I'm not totally sure of the details," Mistress O'Keefe said, "but it appears that he was wandering along the harbour front at night with a lantern – goodness only knows why – and he was caught by the revenue men who accused him of being a wrecker."

McDougal clenched his fists and spoke through gritted teeth. "I've always had my doubts about Burgess, but I doubt that even he would be that stupid. My guess is that the revenue men are probably looking for a scapegoat – someone they can make an example of – and he was an easy target for a trumped-up charge. And it must be a trumped-up charge, because whatever else we might have done, we've never been wreckers. But whatever has happened, we must all work together now to get him acquitted – for our own sakes as well as his."

He squared his shoulders and looked around the room. "I will hire the best barrister we can find. But in the meantime, we must make sure that nothing – I repeat, nothing – can possibly be found here if the revenue men come searching. Come, young Heathcliff; it's time to make a bit more use of that priest-hole. And Mistress O'Keefe, is the trapdoor in good working order?"

"Trapdoor?" I asked, feeling both amazed and alarmed.

"It's just inside the front door," McDougal explained, "and drops down into the cellar. It's our secret weapon. We've never needed to use it so far, and Heaven forbid that we ever should, but it is good to be prepared."

He then turned back to Mistress O'Keefe. "I think you can help us immensely in this."

"I, Mr McDougal? But what can I do to help?"

"Much more than you imagine. All along, the revenue men have only been looking for men. As I've always said, they'll never suspect a woman. So, this is what you need to do…"

***

Mary O'Keefe

"Judge Collingwood! Please, come in out of the cold."

71

Today is Mr Burgess's trial, and for once, I blessed the inclement weather. It made my prescribed task so much easier.

The judge walked into The Mermaid, where I helped him off with his sodden cloak and hat and hung them up to dry.

"May I offer you a warm drink, Your Honour?" I glanced towards the window and grimaced at the sight of the torrential rain and howling wind outside.

He hesitated, but on following my gaze, he capitulated with a grateful smile. "Thank you, Mistress O'Keefe. You are most kind."

"Please excuse me for a moment, Your Honour. The hot spiced ale is in the kitchen, keeping warm on the stove."

I took one of the tankards from the bar and made my way into the kitchen. I ladled some of the hot liquid into the tankard, then, making sure I was well out of sight of the serving area, I added a generous jigger of strong French brandy. Taking a good sniff of the steam to check that the aroma of the alcohol was well and truly masked by the powerful scent of the cinnamon and cloves, I returned to the bar and laid the mug on the counter.

The judge picked up the mug and surrounded it with his hands, savouring its heat, before taking a deep breath and inhaling the warm fumes.

"How much do I owe you, Mistress O'Keefe?" he asked.

It was on the tip of my tongue to say that he owed me nothing, but I realised just in time that this might well make him suspicious. And, in any case, why should I not allow him to pay for what I had just served – even if he remained in blissful ignorance of the mug's true contents?

"Just twopence, please, Your Honour."

He laid the mug aside and placed two pennies on the counter.

"Thank you, Your Honour." Pulling up one of the most comfortable chairs and positioning it next to the fire, I motioned him to be seated.

He quaffed the contents of his tankard in three or four gulps, then leaned forward towards the fire and warmed his hands.

"May I refill your tankard?" I asked him.

He looked out of the window at the driving rain, then pulled out his watch from the pocket of his waistcoat and glanced at it. "I am not due at the courthouse for another hour, and I would much rather spend the intervening time here, in this warm congenial atmosphere, than out there in the cold and wet. Yes, please."

"Thank you, Your Honour. And would you care for a slice of gingerbread to go with your drink? I am trying out a new recipe, and would be most grateful for your opinion. There will be no charge for that, of course."

It was indeed a new recipe, but the difference this time was that it was made without my secret ingredient: the very same French brandy with which I had just fortified his tankard of ale. Incorporating the brandy into the cake was a simple and discreet means of keeping it hidden from the revenue men. But today, knowing the task with which I had been entrusted, I had baked a separate, brandy-free batch especially for this purpose. The brandy was what gave the gingerbread its particular flavour and texture, but I had no wish to arouse the judge's suspicions by possibly drawing his attention to it. Aside from this, I was also interested to see if the absence of the brandy made any noticeable difference to the end result.

I handed him the platter and he helped himself to a slice. For the sake of appearances, I also took one myself.

"What do you think, Your Honour?" I asked, when his portion was reduced to no more than a few small crumbs.

He nodded appreciatively as he chewed the final mouthful. "It is very good. Very good indeed."

I took his empty tankard back into the kitchen and replenished the contents. This time, however, I increased the proportion of the brandy. When this tankard too stood empty, I refilled it without his having to ask. And again, and again...

By the time he stood up to leave, the weather had improved slightly. It was still cold and windy, but thankfully the rain had stopped. I was relieved, as it meant that the next stage of the plan stood a greater chance of succeeding.

He opened the tavern door and winced as the icy blast hit

him full in the face. As he staggered down the road towards the courthouse, his gait was wavering and unsteady. I hoped that anyone who saw him would attribute the cause to the strength and power of the wind, rather than to the strength and quantity of the alcohol with which I had plied him for the past sixty minutes...

***

William McDougal

That idiot Burgess comes to trial today. Well, I've done my best; I've hired the finest barrister in Liverpool to defend him – we still need to save our own skins, if not his. I just hope that Mistress O'Keefe has succeeded with the judge...

***

Mary O'Keefe

"John Joseph Burgess, you are hereby charged that on the night of the third of May last, you did wilfully plot to lure shipping on to the rocks offshore. How do you plead – Guilty or Not Guilty?"

"Not Guilty, my Lord." Mr Burgess spoke calmly, but I could see the fear in his eyes as the prosecuting counsel stood and began his speech.

"My Lord, and gentlemen of the jury, this man standing in the dock before you is charged with the most heinous of crimes. After hearing the evidence presented to this court, it is for you to decide if he is guilty of the offence whereof he stands accused. I call my first witness."

His first witness was a man I recognised as one of the revenue men who come to The Mermaid from time to time. He gave his name as Charles Faulkner, and his occupation as Customs Official.

"Mr Faulkner, you are the person who arrested the accused?"

"Yes, sir."

"Please, Mr Faulkner, tell the court what happened."

"I was patrolling the waterfront on the night of the third of May, and I encountered the accused wandering along the waterfront with a lantern in his hand."

"Were you alone?"

"No, sir. I was with two of my colleagues from the Customs Service. We do not patrol alone."

"Is that for your own safety?"

"Partly, and partly in case we need to make an arrest. We must ensure that the proper procedures are followed."

"Of course. What made you suspect that the accused was acting illegally?"

"It is a well-known fact, sir, that lanterns are used by wreckers to lure ships on to rocks in order to plunder them of their cargo. This cargo is then smuggled ashore and then sold on the black market. We have suspected for some time that smuggling has been going on this area, and we have been keeping a close eye on activities, but until now we have found no direct evidence of any such activity."

"And have you now found this 'direct evidence' which has eluded you until now?"

"Yes, sir."

"Thank you, Mr Faulkner. No further questions at this moment, though I may call you again later."

The prosecuting counsel sat down as the defending counsel rose to his feet.

"Mr Faulkner, please will you describe to the court this 'direct evidence' of which you spoke just now?"

"The fact that the accused was carrying a lantern along the waterfront at night."

The defending counsel raised his eyebrows. "And what other evidence do you have?"

For the first time since stepping into the witness box, Mr Faulkner appeared to lose his air of self-confidence. "Er – that is all the evidence we have at this moment, sir."

"I see. And when you see a man carrying a lantern, does it not occur to you that there might be a perfectly innocent reason for it?"

Mr Faulkner opened his mouth to answer, but no sound

came out. I thought back to Mr McDougal's words – that the revenue men must have been looking for a scapegoat – and realised that he could well be right.

The defending counsel nodded to himself. "Thank you, Mr Faulkner. You may stand down. I now call Mr John Burgess." He turned towards the man in the dock. "Mr Burgess, do you confirm that you were walking along the waterfront on the night of the third of May last?"

"Yes, sir, that is true."

"Were you indeed carrying a lantern?"

"Yes, sir."

"Why was that?"

"It was dark, and there was no moon. I needed the lantern so that I could see where I was going."

"And where were you going at that time of night?"

Mr Burgess hesitated, then answered in a low voice, "I was searching for a doctor."

A murmur went round the court.

"Why was that, Mr Burgess?" the defending counsel asked gently.

"My daughter is sick, sir."

Out of the corner of my eye I caught sight of Mr McDougal. His face registered shock, quickly followed by an expression of sudden comprehension.

***

William McDougal

His daughter is sick? Oh, what a blind fool I have been for all this time! Why in Heaven's name did he not tell me?

***

Mary O'Keefe

The next witness to be called was Heathcliff. As he stood in the witness box and took the oath, his face was expressionless.

"Please state your full name," the prosecutor began.

"Heathcliff."

76

"I said, state your full name."

"That is my full name, sir. It is the only name I have ever known."

The prosecutor looked puzzled. "Why do you say that?"

"It has served me as both first name and surname for almost as long as I can recall."

The prosecutor's eyebrows rose. "Almost as long as you can recall? Please, tell me more."

Heathcliff squared his shoulders and stared the prosecutor in the eye. He spoke calmly and clearly.

"I was adopted as a small child by a man called Mr Earnshaw, who took me to his home in the West Riding of Yorkshire and brought me up as his own, alongside his own son and daughter. He and his wife gave me the name of Heathcliff in memory of another son of theirs who had died in infancy."

"Do you have any memory, or knowledge, of the time before you were adopted by this gentleman?"

"No, sir. I have no memory of the time before he took me in, and if I had another name before that, I have no knowledge of what it might have been."

"When did you come to Liverpool?"

"A little less than a year ago."

"And why was that?"

If, like me, Heathcliff was wondering why these questions should have any relevance to the case, he nonetheless gave a straightforward answer.

"Mr Earnshaw died, and the property passed to his son, who had never liked me, and who now made it very clear to me that I was no longer welcome there. I needed to get away and make a fresh start somewhere else."

"What made you decide to come to Liverpool, rather than going anywhere else?"

"I boarded the first coach I found. I came to Liverpool simply because that is where the coach happened to be going."

The prosecuting counsel seemed satisfied with that response, and moved on to the case in hand.

"Tell me, Mr Heathcliff, how do you know the accused,

John Joseph Burgess?"

"I met him at The Mermaid tavern, sir, shortly after I first arrived in Liverpool."

"Do you know him well?"

"Not very well, sir. I have played cards with him at The Mermaid from time to time, but nothing more than that."

"Would you regard him as trustworthy?"

"I have never had any reason to suppose otherwise. As I say, I have played cards with him on occasions, and he has always played honestly and has never attempted to cheat."

"The accused claims that at the time when he was arrested, he was searching for a doctor to attend his sick daughter. Do you believe his story?"

"He has told me of his daughter's illness in the past, sir. I have no reason to doubt that he was telling the truth."

"Thank you, Mr Heathcliff. You may stand down. I next call Mistress Mary O'Keefe."

***

William McDougal

Young Heathcliff was a model of discretion. The only thing which puzzled me was his claim that Burgess had already told him about his daughter being sick. I wonder why neither of them had ever mentioned it to me?

***

Mary O'Keefe

I took my place in the witness box and was handed a well-worn copy of the Bible. Repeating the words of the oath, I swore to tell the truth, the whole truth and nothing but the truth.

To tell the truth, I was nervous.

The prosecuting counsel turned to me. "Please, madam, state your full name."

"Mary Elizabeth O'Keefe."

"And you are the proprietor of The Mermaid Tavern?"

"Yes, sir."

"Now please, Mistress O'Keefe, look at the man standing in the dock, John Joseph Burgess. Do you recognise him?"

"Yes, sir."

"And how do you know him?"

I drew a deep breath. "Sir, he is a customer at my tavern."

There was no point in pretending otherwise. I had no doubt that there would be plenty of witnesses (including the revenue men) who would confirm that John Burgess had been seen at The Mermaid on numerous occasions.

"How often does he come to your tavern?"

"Most evenings, sir."

"And why do you think he comes to your tavern so often?"

It was on the tip of my tongue to suggest that the prosecutor might do better to put that question to Burgess himself, but I had no wish to risk angering him. That would achieve nothing, save perhaps to prejudice the case against the man in the dock.

Instead, I answered, in as calm a voice as I could muster: "I believe, sir, that they come because they enjoy the ale I serve."

"And do you also serve food to your customers?"

"I do, sir."

"What kind of food?"

"Stews or soups, mainly, sir, because they are easy to prepare and do not need constant attention. I can keep a pot of soup or stew warm on the stove or by the fire, and serve a portion very quickly if a customer needs one in a hurry."

"I have heard, Mistress O'Keefe, that your soups and stews are particularly fine, and that people travel some distance to consume them. Why do you think this might be?"

I hesitated. The question sounded innocuous enough – so much so that I wondered if it was indeed relevant. But then it occurred to me: was this in fact a loaded question, intended to discover more about the ingredients of my recipes, and how I came by them? How much did the prosecutor suspect?

"Mistress O'Keefe?"

I coughed, to try to disguise my nervousness. "My apologies, sir. I have been suffering from a slight cold, and it still troubles me occasionally."

The prosecutor inclined his head slightly in acknowledgement, then continued, "If you please, Mistress O'Keefe, my question still stands."

"Sir, I am honoured and flattered to think that my cooking should be so popular. As to why that might be, I am afraid I am at a loss to understand. I simply do my best with such ingredients as are available to me at any one time. It is fortunate that the results are usually successful."

"I see." His tone suggested that he was by no means fully convinced, and his next question suggested that he was not prepared to let this matter drop.

"I believe you also bake cakes?"

I could see where this was leading – he was going to ask how I obtained the sugar. This was going to be difficult to answer without giving too much away.

But I was saved from the need to respond by a low rumbling sound coming from the judge's bench above us. It was a few moments before I realised that the sound was that of snoring.

The defending counsel rose to his feet, laid his hand on the prosecutor's arm, and murmured something in his ear as he nodded towards the judge's bench. The prosecutor followed his gaze, frowned, murmured something back, then addressed the court.

"Ladies and gentlemen, the trial is adjourned."

Turning back to me, he told me I was free to leave.

Mr McDougal had previously said that the revenue men would never suspect a woman. Maybe the prosecuting counsel had decided that he had no further use for me, as the testimony of a woman was clearly of no significance.

***

William McDougal

I was worried for a moment, but it looks as though the tide may be turning our way...

***

Leaving the court I noticed that a large crowd had gathered outside, but I paid no heed to them and made my way back to The Mermaid. Although the rain had now stopped, there was still a cold edge to the wind, and by the time I arrived at the tavern I was chilled to the bone. To take my mind off what might be happening down at the courtroom, I decided to keep myself occupied by preparing a large pan of soup. I found the meat stock I'd made the previous day and put it over the fire, and as it heated up I measured out the oatmeal, rice and spices and chopped the onions, celery and carrots. As always, I found that the whole process of pottering around the stove relaxed me and calmed my nerves. Whatever the circumstances, there is always something very satisfying about producing delicious food, whether it is prepared for myself or for others.

The soup was simmering nicely when the front door swung open and Heathcliff strode in.

"What happened?" I asked, as he approached the bar.

Heathcliff grinned. "The trial was abandoned. Well, not so much 'abandoned' as 'came to an early conclusion'."

I was astounded. "What do you mean?"

"You saw that the judge had fallen asleep?"

I nodded. "Saw and heard. I think the whole courtroom could hear him snoring!"

"Well, it turned out that he wasn't just asleep – he was blind drunk. The clerk of the court eventually managed to wake him up, then the defending counsel persuaded him that there wasn't enough evidence to prove anything against Burgess, so the charge was withdrawn. And I can't help wondering if that crowd outside might have had something to do with it as well. They certainly looked menacing enough."

The judge was blind drunk? So my role in this sorry business must have succeeded after all.

"How is Mr Burgess?" I asked.

"I didn't speak to him after the trial ended, but I believe he's on his way here, with Mr McDougal." Heathcliff grinned again. "And I think when they arrive, they will both be in need

81

of some of your finest ale." He sniffed the air. "And some of that soup, too, I'll wager."

It was only a few minutes later that the door crashed open and Mr McDougal and Mr Burgess entered. The latter looked pale and weary, but his eyes shone with relief. Mr McDougal helped him to a seat then called for ale. I brought two brimming tankards to their table, followed by two bowls of soup. Heathcliff joined them, armed with a full tankard and bowl of his own.

I returned to the bar and gave the soup another stir, then threw in a surreptitious dash of Madeira wine. Today was a day for celebration.

**

Autumn 1781

William McDougal

I think it's about time Burgess did something other than just land-gang stuff, to take his mind off his other problems. He claims he's no sailor, but it must be close to ten years since that business with the press gang, so I would hope he might be a bit more amenable to the idea by now. I'll have a word with Trelawney and see if he can take him on one of the Roscoff runs.

**

John Burgess

Little Emily is still weak, but, praise Heaven, she is no worse. Bill McDougal has been kindness itself since the trial. Many a time he has berated me (in a friendly way) for not telling him sooner about her illness.

But he has now asked me to go with Trelawney and young Heathcliff on one of their sea trips. I haven't set foot on a ship for nigh on ten years, and the prospect still fills me with nothing but dread. But after he's been so good to me, how can I refuse?

**

Matthew Trelawney

Bill McDougal wants me to take John Burgess with us next time we go to Roscoff. He reckons the fellow needs a change of scenery. I must admit I have some misgivings about this, but I suppose I'll have to go along with it for now. I'll get young Heathcliff to keep an eye on him. As far as I can tell, Burgess seems quite fond of the lad.

***

Heathcliff

Trelawney told me today that we'll be off to Roscoff again in a couple of days. McDougal wants us to take John Burgess with us this time, and Trelawney has asked me to look after him. I wonder why McDougal has decided this all of a sudden? I'd always thought that Burgess was afraid of sailing – and as Trelawney has said so often, our business has no room for passengers.

***

John Burgess

We set sail in a few hours. I wish I could say I was looking forward to this. McDougal has promised me that he'll keep a close eye on my family whilst I'm away, but all the same, I'm still worried about leaving them.

***

Heathcliff

Trelawney had warned me before we set sail that Burgess was nervous about coming on board, so I had to think of ways to keep him distracted. I thought back to what Trelawney had said to me on my first voyage with him, so I began by asking Burgess if he felt all right.

"In what way, lad?" he said. I must confess his answer took me slightly by surprise; until then, it hadn't occurred to me

83

that he might have other concerns than just seasickness.

"Are you feeling seasick?"

"Seasick? I don't feel too bad at the moment, thank you, though what will happen when we get out into open sea remains to be seen. But for now, that's the least of my worries." He suddenly fell silent, as though he had said more than he intended.

"May I ask why?" I asked, in what I hoped was a friendly tone. "Is it your daughter?"

Burgess hesitated, staring out across the water, then turned to face me.

"Yes, in part, but that isn't the whole story. I don't usually talk about it, as it all happened so long ago, but I suppose you might as well know. Everyone else does, and it's probably better that you hear it from me, rather than some second- or third-hand version that's been distorted over time."

I was intrigued. "What happened?"

"Have you heard of the press gang?"

"No. Who are they, and what do they do?"

Burgess looked surprised at my response, but he went on to explain. "They're gangs of thugs who see it as their job to swell the ranks of the navy. But their methods are far from honest. In short, they kidnap men and force them to go to sea. One of their favourite tricks is to pretend to befriend men in taverns, ply them with drink, then drop a shilling in their victim's tankard. The victim only finds it when he's finished the ale, and by then it's too late because the shilling is regarded as the man's property. That's their way of conning him into 'taking the King's shilling' – in other words, signing up to join the navy. Around ten years ago, they caught me."

"Oh my goodness. What happened? Did you escape?"

"McDougal came to my rescue. He told them that he was my doctor, and that I was very sick and would be no use at all as a sailor. He got me back to The Mermaid (by a very long way round, so eventually they grew tired of trying to follow us), and Mistress O'Keefe hid me in a secret room in the attic."

"The priest-hole?"

Burgess nodded. "I was concealed up there for almost a week. Mistress O'Keefe kept me supplied with food and drink." He grimaced. "I only emerged when I had to use the privy – and only then when she assured me that it was safe. Then, eventually, McDougal came up and told me I could come out. It seemed that he'd met the gang again, and they'd asked him how his patient was faring. He managed to convince them that I'd died of whatever illness I was supposed to be suffering from."

"What?"

"Yes. Then he asked me if I wanted to join his land-gang. Since he'd saved me from becoming a pressed man, what could I do but accept?" He sighed, and stared out to sea. "I owe him so much, though I know I've not repaid him very well over the years. But since then, I've always had a dreadful fear of ships." He turned back towards me and forced a smile. "But that's more than enough about me. Tell me about you."

But before I could answer, the ship lurched as it hit a wave, and Burgess turned a ghastly shade of greenish-white, doubled over and clasped his middle. I grabbed his arm and propelled him to the starboard rail. Once he had emptied the contents of his stomach into the sea, he straightened up and looked at me, shamefaced.

"I did warn them all that I wasn't a very good sailor."

I patted his arm. "Don't worry – you'll soon find your sea-legs. In the meantime, focus on the horizon. That's what Trelawney told me when I first sailed with him, and it really does help."

After his first bout of seasickness Burgess seemed to recover, and the remainder of the voyage passed without further incident. The weather was kind to us, and we completed the round trip in just under six days. In fact, once he'd become accustomed to life on board, he appeared almost to enjoy it at times – though, occasionally, I caught him staring out to sea, lost in thought.

***

John Burgess

That was an interesting trip, and quite enjoyable once I'd got over my fear of sailing. And McDougal had looked after the family very well whilst I was away. I'd have no objection to doing another trip, if they're happy to have me on board.

***

Heathcliff

Burgess has now done four of the Roscoff runs, and it now appears that he is to accompany us on our next triangular trip. I don't know how much he knows about what happens during these trips, but Trelawney has asked me to look after him. Presumably by that he means 'look after him' in the same sense that Trelawney himself looked after me during my first triangular trip. I'll do my best, but I don't think anything can really prepare anyone for the full horrors of what's in store. To be honest, I'm not even sure myself if I'll find it better or worse the second time around.

***

John Burgess

McDougal has now asked me to go with Trelawney and Heathcliff on a much longer voyage. The trips to and from Roscoff have only taken around a week in total, but this one will last for several months. I am not sure I want to be away for such a long time; little Emily is still frail, and Anne is now four months gone with child. But once again, I don't see how I can refuse.

***

Heathcliff

We set sail from Liverpool yesterday. Trelawney told me privately that this time we will be travelling to America rather than Barbados. The customer there has requested fewer slaves than we had on the previous trip, so he plans to fill up the extra space in the hold with African elephant ivory. This, too, promises a healthy profit, both in America and back home.

I think Burgess is still a little apprehensive about the long voyage. Although he fared quite well on the Roscoff trips, I can tell that he's not really looking forward to being away from his family for months on end. From what I've heard, his daughter seems to be better (or at least, no worse), but I can see that he's still worried about her. He told me that on the night when he was arrested she had a high fever, and it was little short of a miracle that she survived. McDougal has promised to make sure she gets proper care whilst Burgess is away, but all the same, I don't think he's convinced it's a good idea to go away for so long. And as if he didn't already have enough to think about, it transpires that his wife is once again with child. Four months gone, he says. Whatever that means.

I asked him what he meant. He looked a little embarrassed, but took it upon himself to explain to me how his wife came to be with child. I was both shocked and ashamed at how little I realised I knew. During my time working on the land at The Heights, I had observed how the animals mated and produced young, but I had never previously applied this same knowledge to men and women. Even after observing how some of the crew had used and abused the female slaves during the crossing to Barbados, I had still not associated this with childbirth.

It seems that babies take a ninemonth in the making, and now I find myself wondering how many of those female slaves went on to bear children a few months after they had been sold in the slave market in Bridgetown.

***

John Burgess

When I told young Heathcliff that my wife was four months gone with child, he looked puzzled.

"I am sorry," he said, "but what do you mean by that?"

It seems that the lad's knowledge of the facts of life is

87

rudimentary, to say the least of it. I never imagined that I would be the one who would have to tell him.

After my explanation, he told me how he came to be involved with McDougal's gang. He came to Liverpool to escape from a girl who broke his heart. I've always thought he seemed like a troubled soul. Now, I think I understand why.

***

Heathcliff

As before, the first part of the voyage has been most enjoyable. Burgess seemed constantly in awe (as indeed I was on my first trip) of the changing scenery, the warm weather and the delights of the Portuguese and Madeiran food and wine. He even claimed to enjoy the confounded dried codfish, though how much longer his kind opinion will last remains to be seen. Poor fellow – he has absolutely no idea that things are about to get an awful lot worse.

***

John Burgess

We've just left the island of Madeira and are heading south towards Africa. The weather is becoming steadily hotter.

Young Heathcliff has told me that when we arrive on the west coast of Africa we will exchange our cargo for a consignment of slaves. These will be transported across to America to work on the tobacco plantations in Maryland and Virginia.

I knew that our tobacco came from the Americas, but I had no idea that it was produced using slave labour.

Oh dear God. What on earth have I taken on?

***

Heathcliff

Since I explained to Burgess what will happen next, he's barely said a word to anyone on board. I'm beginning to wonder if McDougal (or Trelawney) ever gave him any advance warning of what the voyage would involve.

We're now approaching the Slave Coast and should arrive in Lagos tomorrow. Burgess looks terrified.

***

John Burgess

When we arrived in Lagos, we were greeted by a man whom Trelawney introduced as Senhor da Costa, who (Heathcliff explained to me) was a business associate of Bill McDougal. He led us to his house just outside the village, and gave us refreshments – a most pleasant change after the monotony of our diet at sea. The fresh fruits from his garden, and the sharp drink made from locally-grown lemons, were especially welcome.

"And now, Senhor Trelawney, to business! I have some particularly fine specimens for you this time. How many do you require?"

Trelawney produced a paper from his waistcoat pocket and consulted it. "Our customers in America have requested one hundred in total."

Senhor da Costa appeared troubled. "Only one hundred? But I have twice that quantity at your disposal! Can you find room for more?"

Trelawney scratched his chin and appeared to consider this proposal. "At what price?" he asked, after a moment.

"One hundred slaves would cost you two pounds each, but if you were to take two hundred, the price would come down to one pound fifteen shillings each."

Trelawney considered again. "If you are prepared to shake hands on one pound twelve shillings and sixpence, we have a deal."

Senhor da Costa made as if to argue further, but then shrugged his shoulders and extended his hand. "You drive a hard bargain, Senhor Trelawney. But one pound twelve shillings and sixpence it is."

"Where on earth are we going to accommodate two hundred

people?" I whispered to Heathcliff.

His response shook me to the core. "We mustn't think of them as people. They are cargo, and they travel as cargo."

***

Heathcliff

Once again, I was given the task of handing out the slaves' daily rations. I engaged Burgess to help me with this. As there were considerably fewer slaves this time, and the workload was shared between two of us rather than falling to me alone, this meant that we had rather more free time than I had enjoyed on my first trip.

Burgess performed his duties in silence, as if he were trying to distance himself from the whole business. But he was involved in one particular incident which took me completely by surprise.

We were around three weeks into the crossing. During one of our routine visits to the slave deck, we became aware of a commotion in the enclosure which housed the women and children.

One of the women was lying on her back and screaming. She was drenched with sweat, her stomach was grotesquely swollen, and blood was pooling around her lower regions. I wondered if she was suffering from the bloody flux, but Burgess shook his head, seized my arm and dragged me to one side.

"We need to summon the doctor. Her child is coming."

"Her child?" I gasped. "How do you know?"

"I have a child of my own, remember? I've seen this before. Come on – there is no time to lose."

He rushed to the upper deck. I followed, eventually catching up with him as he spoke to Doctor Hamilton.

"You need to come now. One of the women is in labour."

I wondered what Burgess meant by 'in labour' – I had only ever heard the word associated with working on the farm – but I decided that this was probably not the best moment to ask.

Doctor Hamilton grabbed his medical bag and we made our

way back down to the slave deck. As I unlocked the women's enclosure and he entered, the other inmates stood aside to let him pass. Somehow they seemed to sense that he was there to help the poor woman who was lying in agony on the ground. She could not understand English, and we had no idea what tongue she or her companions were speaking, but screams of pain are the same in any language.

"She needs air," Doctor Hamilton said. "And space. Can we get her out of this cage? Don't move her further than you have to, but she can't give birth in here."

Burgess nodded and put his hands under the woman's shoulders. "Come on, Heathcliff. You take her feet."

I hesitated. Surely it was not my place to take any part in this painful (and, in truth, highly embarrassing) procedure.

"JUST DO IT!" Burgess yelled. "This is no time to be squeamish. You can faint or be sick later."

"Wait until just after her next contraction," Doctor Hamilton said. "They're about two minutes apart, so that should give you plenty of time before the next one. I'll tell you when."

"Contraction?" I whispered to Burgess.

"Pain," he whispered back. His next words were lost as the woman on the ground let out another blood-curdling cry.

"Now!" Doctor Hamilton ordered. As he turned to the other women and gave them a reassuring smile, Burgess and I picked up the woman and manoeuvred her as gently as possible to the area just outside the cage (at a safe distance from where the men were chained). He settled her, half-sitting, half-lying, on the floor, with her knees bent and her back propped up against the timbers of the hull, then knelt down by her feet. Burgess, meanwhile, held her hand and smiled at her, as if in encouragement.

"You seem to know a lot about this," Doctor Hamilton said to Burgess, sounding a little surprised.

"When my wife gave birth to our first child, we could not afford a doctor, so I had to deliver the baby myself," Burgess answered. "Fortunately, I already knew a little about the birthing process, from my work as a farmer. I've helped several calves into the world over the years. In the event, there was not very much difference."

Doctor Hamilton nodded, then then turned to me. "Can you go and get a basin of water and a cloth? And bring a blanket too. Be quick – I don't think it will be much longer now."

In truth, I was not sorry to have an excuse to leave the slave deck. The poor woman would be far better off in the hands of those who, unlike me, knew what to do. But thinking back to what Burgess had told me, I found myself wondering who the father of this child might be. A man from the woman's home tribe, maybe? One thing was certain, though: she had been on board for less than a month, so it could not possibly be one of our own crew.

When I returned with the water, a handkerchief, and an old piece of sailcloth (the nearest thing to a blanket that I'd been able to find), the woman's screams had reached fever-pitch. Burgess grabbed the handkerchief, soaked it in the water and began to mop her face, whilst Doctor Hamilton reached between her legs and made strange up-and-down movements with his shoulders.

"He's trying to tell her to push," Burgess explained, in answer to my quizzical glance. "The child is almost here now."

"Here it comes! The head is born!" Doctor Hamilton announced, before making the strange pushing gesture again. The woman drew a deep breath and screamed again, then the air was pierced by a small, high-pitched cry.

"It's a boy." Doctor Hamilton lifted up the tiny creature and handed it to the mother, who now lay back, panting and exhausted.

"How can you tell?" I whispered to Burgess.

"Just look!" he whispered back, in an exasperated tone. "It's pretty obvious!"

Doctor Hamilton gently covered the mother with the sailcloth. "Go and fetch her some water," he instructed.

"But what about the rations?" I asked.

"Rations?" Doctor Hamilton shouted. "These are exceptional circumstances. This is no time to be worrying about rations!"

It was the first time I have ever seen him angry.

***

John Burgess

Today, a baby boy was born on the slave deck. When I set out on this voyage, I never imagined that I would find myself assisting with a birth.

The child seemed healthy enough, but I fear for the poor mite's future.

***

Matthew Trelawney

I have now added '*One child at breast*' to the register of slaves in our charge. I don't know if this will make the mother less attractive to the buyers, but at least the child is male, so could be of some use longer-term. I've learned from bitter experience that female infants are much more difficult to sell.

***

Heathcliff

The port of Baltimore was a most welcome sight as we sailed into Chesapeake Bay, made our way up the river, and dropped anchor in the harbour. Trelawney signalled towards the shore, and a few minutes later a small rowing-boat made its way towards us and moored alongside. Its passenger, a well-dressed man who I guessed was probably of similar age to old Mr Earnshaw at the time of his death, climbed aboard and shook Trelawney warmly by the hand.

"It is good to see you again, Mr Trelawney!"

"You too, Mr Sullivan! May I introduce my colleagues: Mr Heathcliff and Mr Burgess. And this is Doctor Hamilton."

"It is a pleasure to meet you, gentlemen! Have you had a pleasant voyage?"

'Pleasant' was hardly the word I would have used under the circumstances, but thankfully I was spared the need to answer.

"It was certainly a productive voyage, Mr Sullivan," Trelawney smiled. "A baby boy was born during the crossing."

"Indeed?" He turned to Doctor Hamilton. "Did you attend the lady in question?"

"I did, sir. It was a little over two weeks ago, and I am pleased to report that the mother and the child are both in good health."

"That is good news. Will you all join me for dinner this evening?"

Trelawney answered for all of us. "It would be our pleasure. Thank you."

A few hours later found us seated round the table at Mr Sullivan's home. The house was a little more modest than the mansion in Barbados, but all the same it still made a refreshing change from the confines of the ship.

Mr Sullivan raised his glass and proposed a toast. "To the *Mersey Rose*. her crew, and her associates! May they all continue to prosper!"

I was seated beside Mr Sullivan's daughter, who bore such a striking resemblance to Cathy that I found it quite unnerving. She was of similar age, and had the same brown hair and clear dark eyes. I tried to avoid looking directly at her and would have been happy to have passed the meal in silence, but it seemed that she had other ideas.

"Mr Heathcliff, have you been a sailor for a long time?" she asked, with a winning smile.

"Around a year, Miss Sullivan."

"Please, call me Charlotte. I do not like to stand on ceremony where it is not necessary."

"As you wish." I was surprised at her frankness.

"And what is your first name?"

"I do not have one. I have always been known as just Heathcliff."

"Really?" She raised her eyebrows in surprise. "May I ask why?"

I explained my history, as briefly as possible since I did not wish to bore her, and omitting any details which I feared she might find distasteful. But she seemed genuinely interested in the tale, looking at me throughout with a keen expression in her dark eyes.

"That is a most fascinating story, Heathcliff," she said, when I had finished. "Have you enjoyed your time at sea?"

"It has certainly given me the opportunity for new experiences," I answered carefully.

"Such as?"

"I would never otherwise have visited such exotic locations as Madeira, or Africa, or Barbados. Or, indeed, here!"

"I am very glad that you did." She flashed that winning smile at me again.

Oh Cathy, you used to smile at me like that...

At this point our food was served, and I was extremely grateful for the distraction as we began to eat.

"What is this meat?" I asked her, glad of the opportunity to change the subject.

"It is ham, from Virginia. My uncle owns a tobacco plantation there. Have you not eaten ham before?"

"Yes, back in England, but it tasted nothing like this. I had no idea it could be so different from what I've known."

The ham was not the only thing which seemed sweeter and more tender than what I remembered from life in Yorkshire. After Cathy's rejection, I had always believed that no woman would ever want me. But the charming Miss Sullivan, although she (like Cathy in her new-found status with Edgar Linton) was way above my station, had shown me that I might not be totally lacking in attractiveness after all...

As we took our leave of the Sullivans at the end of the evening, Trelawney (who had been seated opposite me at dinner) seized my arm. He gave the impression of being more than just a little intoxicated.

"Heathcliff, I heard what you were saying earlier to Miss Sullivan about new experiences. I think it's about time you tried another one..."

I glanced around. Burgess and Doctor Hamilton were walking a distance ahead of us, and gave no sign of having heard Trelawney's drunken ramblings.

"Just because one girl broke your heart," Trelawney went on, "that doesn't mean you have to avoid women entirely. There are plenty who are quite happy to show affection to a lonely sailor-boy."

As he steered me through the darkened dockside streets, I couldn't help noticing that many of the houses had red lamps above the doors. I vaguely recalled having seen similar lights back in Liverpool, but I had never thought to wonder what they signified. I was now on the point of finding out.

Trelawney stopped in the middle of the street, looked to and fro at the buildings, then appeared to make a decision (though I have no idea of the reasoning behind it). He led me to one of the front doors and seized the heavy brass knocker. The red lamp cast an eerie, almost unnatural light on us as we waited on the threshold.

The door opened a little, and the head of a surly-looking man emerged through the crack. Trelawney murmured something to him, then handed over some coins, after which the door opened more widely and we were ushered through.

The inside of the house could hardly have been more different from its unassuming exterior. On either side of a wide grand staircase were two large and extravagantly-decorated lounges, each furnished with velvet-covered chairs, enormous mirrors, and a large bar counter at one end. The chairs were occupied by women and girls, all clad only in basques and petticoats.

The doorman clicked his fingers, at which two of the girls rose from their seats and made their way towards us. One clung to Trelawney's arm, the other to mine. Trelawney leaned over to my companion and whispered something in her ear, at which she glanced at me, then looked back to him and nodded.

"She will look after you," he said to me, as the girls began to lead us up the staircase. "There's never a time like the first. Just enjoy it!"

As we reached the top of the stairs, Trelawney and his

companion disappeared through one of the many doors on the landing, whilst my companion steered me to a door at the far end of the corridor. Once inside the room (which was sparsely furnished, with a bed just wide enough for two, a closet, and a table and chair), she turned to me and placed her hands on my shoulders.

"I understand that this is your first time," she said, with a surprising kindness in her voice and compassion in her eyes.

I nodded. For some reason which I couldn't fathom, I felt more than a little ashamed.

"Don't worry," she cooed, taking my hand and leading me towards the bed. "There is a first time for everyone. I will show you what to do…"

That night my youthful inexperience of women came to an end, at the hands of the teacher Trelawney had bought for me. She was young, she was comely, she was knowledgeable, and she was willing.

But she was not Cathy…

The following morning, as we left the house, Trelawney laid a brotherly hand on my arm.

"Did you enjoy it?"

I thought back to the previous night. Once I had recovered from the first bout, I had felt emboldened to try again, and had been surprised by my own prowess. My companion had submitted to me willingly, and had even complimented me on my strength and staying power. I realised that I owed Trelawney thanks for what he had arranged.

"Yes. Thank you. It was quite unlike anything I'd expected, but she was…"

"Good?"

"Yes. She didn't seem to mind that I was a complete novice."

"I knew she'd be all right for you. We all have to start somewhere. And don't worry – the girls here are all clean. No danger of the pox."

In the heat of the moment I had not given this matter a

thought – nor had it occurred to me to wonder if there might be other consequences of what we had done. Burgess's explanation about the begetting of infants came unbidden to my mind.

"What about…babies?" I asked, hoping that I sounded less afraid than I felt.

Trelawney shook his head. "No need to concern yourself with that. The girls have their own ways of dealing with it."

I didn't like to ask what he meant by that, but I was curious to know more about the other matter.

"You mentioned the pox where we were in Barbados. How do you catch it, and what is so dreadful about it?"

Trelawney's face grew serious. "You catch it by coupling with a woman who has it. Once you've caught it, it's incurable, and you will pass it on to anyone else you couple with. It will ruin your life, and eventually it will kill you. Some men go completely insane. Others find their personalities change beyond all recognition. And if you have children, it can affect them too."

"Really? In what way?"

"All sorts of ways. The child could end up blind, or deaf, or just with poor health in general. All the more reason to avoid it."

I shuddered. "How do you know if you've got it?"

"For a long time, you don't. You might eventually start to get sores which won't go away, but some people never get any symptoms at all." He squared his shoulders and drew himself up to his full height. "But that's enough of such gloomy talk. Time to go and see how much our cargo is worth."

***

Matthew Trelawney

I didn't like to tell young Heathcliff that all bawdy-houses are much the same, with all the same risks. I'm happy to let him go on thinking this particular one was special. I only chose it because it happened to be the one I visited when I first came to Baltimore. It was a great solace after Louise jilted me.

I hope it helped him too – I get the impression he's still upset, even now, about what happened with his girl back in England.

Sullivan told me this morning that the market for slaves here is just as lively as ever. It seems that a lot of slaves joined the army during the Revolutionary War, and some of the slaves here in Baltimore have since become craftsmen, sailors, journeymen, and domestic servants. But the plantation owners in Virginia still need plenty. So although our cargo was considerably smaller than what we took to Barbados, it still brought us a healthy profit of around ten thousand pounds. McDougal should be content enough with that.

***

John Burgess

Doctor Hamilton and I became separated from Trelawney and Heathcliff after we left the Sullivans yesterday evening, and I didn't see them again until this morning. They both looked somewhat the worse for wear, but Trelawney in particular seemed to be in good spirits. He told me that we've made a good profit on this trip, and once the ship is cleaned out (which should take two or three days), we can load up with our cargo of tobacco.

I must confess to being more than a little shocked by what I've experienced on this trip. Not just the way the slaves were transported, but also by young Heathcliff's attitude. As we were approaching Africa, he took me aside and said something which made my blood run cold:

"When I first did this trip, Trelawney gave me a piece of advice: Harden your heart. And that's what you have to do. It's the only way you'll get through it. You just have to convince yourself not to think of them as people. They're a cargo which needs to be kept in good condition until it reaches its destination."

I had hitherto thought of young Heathcliff as a troubled soul with a broken heart. But now I'm beginning to wonder if this whole business is turning him into a hard-hearted brute.

***

Summer 1782

Heathcliff

I have returned from this voyage far more enriched than I ever anticipated. And I am not referring solely to money.

***

September 1783

Heathcliff

I joined Trelawney on the *Mersey Rose* for two further triangular trips: one to Barbados and one to Baltimore, where we made several more visits to his favourite bawdy-house. As before, the girls were comely, willing, and very experienced.. The evenings were expensive (I had no idea, until then, how much it must have cost Trelawney to pay for both of us on my first visit), but we were wealthy enough for our enjoyment not to make too great a hole in our coffers.

By now, I have amassed a significant fortune. How it has been acquired is something which I have pushed firmly to the back of my mind.

I have also learned how to distance myself emotionally from what I have been doing. Trelawney's motto *Harden your heart* has been my lifeline throughout this whole episode. I think my heart has become harder with each passing voyage. Otherwise, I don't think I could have survived.

But we have heard rumours that moves are afoot to outlaw the slave trade. It may not happen immediately, but perhaps the time has now come for me to close this chapter of my life and return to Yorkshire. Who knows, my new-found riches might yet prove to win Cathy's hand, if I am not too late to prevent her from marrying Linton.

I sought out McDougal at the earliest opportunity, and told him of my decision.

"I shall miss you," he replied, "but I will not stand in your

100

way."

"Thank you. But before I leave, please may I ask you something?"

"Of course."

"You've told me you're a Catholic, and I can see how devout you are. Yet so much that you do seems to be outside the law. Why is that?"

McDougal grinned. "My allegiance is to a far higher cause than the laws of this land. As you already know, I have no respect for those laws, nor for the upstart impostor who makes them."

"But what about your beliefs?" I asked, recalling what the Bible-bashing curate at Gimmerton had taught us about saints and sinners. "Do you believe in Heaven and Hell?"

His face grew serious. "I believe in Heaven, for sure. But I've never believed any of that talk of Hell. The priests tried to scare us with talk of 'eternal fire', but my mother always taught me to think of God as a loving and forgiving father. So when I do face my maker, I know that all my sins will be forgiven. Anyone who's ever had a child will know that a parent's love is unconditional. So I don't for one moment believe that a loving God would ever condemn his own creation."

I thought again of John Burgess and how devoted he was to his sick daughter (who continued to cling on to life despite her failing health) and his young son who had been born a few weeks after our return from our first trip to America. But I found it impossible to imagine myself in the same position. Thanks to Burgess's advice during the voyage and Trelawney's generosity in Baltimore, I now knew exactly what the process involved. But unless my darling Cathy changed her mind about marrying Edgar Linton, I was still sure that I would never become a father myself.

But then, this talk of parents caused me to wonder about my own background.

Nelly, I recalled, had said I should "frame high notions of my birth"; that I should imagine that my father was a Chinese emperor and my mother an Indian queen, with wealth enough between them to buy up Wuthering Heights and Thrushcross Grange together, and that I'd been kidnapped by wicked sailors and brought to England. But after my experiences in Baltimore, coupled with what I now knew of my surroundings in Liverpool, I deduced that it was far more likely that my mother had been a lady of the night who worked in one of the many dockside bawdy-houses, and my father a sailor who had been desperate for a brief spell of female company during a period of shore leave. In which case, my mother (whoever she was) might not even have known his name. Never in a thousand years could either of these notions be described as high. In any case, I don't suppose I will ever find out.

Maybe being brought to The Heights by Mr Earnshaw was the best I could have hoped for. I have very little memory of what happened (I was no more than four or five years old at the time), and even less memory of my life before that. But some years later, when I was old enough to understand, he'd told me of how he'd found me wandering the streets of Liverpool. I was dirty, ragged and starving, and could not even speak properly or understand what he said to me. Goodness knows what would have happened to me if he hadn't taken me under his wing. I probably wouldn't even have seen my tenth birthday.

McDougal seized my hand and pressed it with a firm, comradely handshake. "God-speed, young man."

"Thank you for everything you have done for me." I whispered. "You have nothing to fear – your secret is safe with me. Nobody will ever know about you, or your various ventures, or how I came by my fortune."

"Thank you. I'm so pleased that I've been able to help you. As I've said, you feel like the son I never had. But even after giving you your share of the profits, I still have far more money than I could ever need for myself, so I am proposing to use some of it to help a more worthy cause." He smiled, raised his tankard and solemnly clinked it with mine. "A final toast: to the King over the Water."

I nodded and smiled back at him. "To the King over the Water."

I feared his dream was far more of a lost cause than a worthy one, but I would not be the one to dash his hopes.

PART THREE

RETURN

(1783)

Liverpool

September 1783

Thomas Braithwaite, Coachman

I did not recognise the man at first. He was well-dressed, well-mannered and well-spoken. It was only when he asked me if I recalled our first meeting, a little over three years ago, that I finally realised who he was.

"Forgive me, sir," I said. "You are much changed since that day."

He nodded and gave a strange smile. "I am well aware of that."

"What brings you here today?"

"I wish to return to Yorkshire. Are you heading in that direction, and do you have space in your coach?"

"I am, sir, and I do. The fare will be eight shillings and sixpence for an inside seat."

He pulled a sovereign from his pocket and dropped it into my hand. "I recall that three years ago you were good enough to transport me here, out of the kindness of your heart, for only a few pence. This should cover the cost of both that journey and this one."

I was dumbfounded, and made as if to protest, but he held up a hand for silence.

"Never let it be said that I do not settle my debts," he said.

I thanked him for his generosity, and he acknowledged my thanks with a nod, but I discerned in his eyes a strange gleam which made me feel very uneasy. I found myself wondering if he had other 'debts', possibly of a non-monetary nature, which he also wished to settle.

Was this why he was now heading back to his former home?

***

Gimmerton, The Yorkshire Moors

September 1783

Heathcliff

When I first arrived back at The Heights and knocked on the door, I heard cursing and swearing from within before it was eventually opened. It was a few moments before I realised that the man standing – or rather slouching – on the threshold was none other than Hindley.

I was shocked at his shabby appearance and wretched demeanour. At first he didn't seem to recognise me at all. But then, I've probably changed quite a bit since he last saw me, and three years is a long time to spend with only alcohol for company. His wife had died two years before I'd left, and even then he was already sinking further and further into dissipation and squalor.

But to my surprise, he invited me in and offered me a drink. And he soon brightened up when I proposed that we should play a hand of cards – for money. He lost, but immediately wanted to play again. And again. By the end of the fifth game (at which point he invited me to lodge with him at The Heights), it was clear to me that he had more than just the one addiction. I must confess to feeling some degree of malicious pleasure in seeing how low he had fallen.

But I still needed to find out about Cathy. Was there still hope that she might have seen sense and called off her engagement, or had she indeed married that idiot Linton? I knew it would be unwise of me to ask Hindley outright about her, so instead I enquired after Nelly. Hindley told me gruffly that he'd sent her to live at The Grange with Cathy and Edgar, following their marriage a couple of months ago.

I was devastated. The past three years had made me rich, successful and worldly-wise – a far cry from the penniless uneducated farmhand whom Cathy had so cruelly rejected. If only I had returned a few months earlier, I might have been able to persuade her that marriage to me might not be so degrading after all.

Now she can never be mine. So what is the point of going on living? I cannot live without my soul.

But I knew I must have one last sight of her. I decided to go to The Grange to see her – even if only at a distance – after which I would return to The Heights, settle my score with Hindley, then end my own life. The past three years had taught me to have even less respect for the law than I had before I left, so my final act would be to cheat the hangman's noose and be my own executioner.

That same evening I made my way to The Grange. But when I arrived my courage failed me. For around an hour I waited in the porch, concealed by the shadows, looking up at the lighted windows and hoping to catch a glimpse of Cathy inside the house. But then I saw a figure approaching from the darkness of the garden. The figure, a woman, was carrying a basket of apples. As she drew closer, I realised who she must be.

"Nelly, is that you?" I asked, stepping out of the shadows.

Nelly gasped, and for some moments appeared transfixed with shock. Once I had convinced her that I was indeed returned, fully flesh and blood and not merely a ghostly vision from the past, she held up her hands in amazement. The basket of apples fell to the ground.

"Is your mistress at home? I would speak with her. Go and tell her that a person from Gimmerton wishes to see her."

"But how will she take it when she sees you?" Nelly answered. "You have changed so much! Have you been a soldier?"

But I was in no mood for such idle chatter. In any case, what had befallen me during the past three years was no concern of hers.

"Go and deliver my message," I persisted. "I am in hell until you do."

***

Nelly Dean

What a shock I had this evening. I had been harvesting some apples from the garden and was bringing them back to the house, when I was accosted in the kitchen porch by a tall man with dark hair, dark whiskers and swarthy skin. At first I did not recognise him. Even when he addressed me by name – which in itself shocked me to the core – his voice sounded unfamiliar, and slightly foreign in tone.

It was some moments before I realised who he was: Heathcliff.

But what a change in him. He was no longer the surly, disheveled, penniless farmhand who had left without a word three years earlier. Here before me stood a well-spoken, well-dressed and prosperous gentleman.

He asked me if the mistress was at home, and bade me tell her that "a person from Gimmerton" wished to see her. I was reluctant to carry out his bidding, as I was afraid how she might react. The sight of him had been shocking enough for me, so I could only begin to imagine what effect it would have on her.

But he was most insistent. He came indoors with me, but waited just inside the kitchen door as I made my way to the parlour.

Mr and Mrs Linton were sitting together in the window-seat, and they both looked so happy and contented that my courage failed me. How could I deliver a message which I knew had the power shatter their peace and harmony for ever?

***

Edgar Linton

Oh merciful Heaven. What a catastrophe has occurred.

That ruffian Heathcliff has returned! Yet he appears much improved, both in manners and in appearance. Indeed, he could even pass for a gentleman. His clothes and his demeanour give every impression of being those of a rich man. If this is so, I cannot begin to imagine how he acquired this new-found wealth. I would be prepared to wager that it could not have been entirely by honest means.

But that is the least of my concerns at this juncture. What worries me far more is how Catherine responded to seeing him. She was beyond overjoyed, and appeared far more animated than I have seen her for many months. It was as though a light had come on in her soul.

I had thought – and had even dared to hope – that she might have forgotten him. We have been so happy together since our wedding. But who knows what will happen now?

***

Catherine Linton (previously Catherine Earnshaw)

Oh, joy of joys – Heathcliff has come back! And what a change in him! He stands proud and tall, his voice has lost its earlier roughness, and he seems successful and prosperous. I would fain have asked him how he had been spending the three years since he left us, but there will be plenty of time for that in the months and years to come. For now, I am content merely that he has returned. He told us he is staying at The Heights with Hindley, so he should be able to visit us often.

My life is complete at last. I have my soulmate back, and I will not lose him again. I'm sure that he and Edgar will become good friends in the fullness of time.

But I am worried about Isabella. All the while he was with us, her gaze never left him, and I am afraid she may be starting to entertain some wild romantic fantasy about him. I sincerely hope not, for everyone's sakes. A more unsuitable pairing would be hard to imagine.

***

Heathcliff

Cathy seemed overjoyed to see me, though Linton was anything but. Outwardly, he was civil enough to me, probably for her sake, but I could tell that underneath it all he was seething. I have to say that my opinion of him has not

111

improved.

At first, Cathy berated me for having been "absent and silent for three years" and never having thought of her. It was hard to contain my anger at such a greeting, but I replied that I had thought of her far more than she could have thought of me during that time, that I had fought through a bitter life, and had struggled only for her. At that, she softened, and I once again saw the smile I have loved and missed for so long.

After witnessing how much my homecoming meant to her, I knew I could no longer carry out my original plan. Heartbreaking though it will be for me to see her married to someone so dreadfully unworthy of her, I realised that I would have to go on living. Which meant I would also have to allow that brute Hindley to go on living.

But as I made my way back to The Heights, a better plan began to form in my mind. I had already discovered Hindley's twin addictions – drink and gambling – and I realised I could probably turn these to my own advantage.

And Linton's silly sister Isabella spent the entire evening making sheep's eyes at me, reminding me of the admiring glances I had once received from the charming Charlotte Sullivan. It then occurred to me that I might be able to make good use of this, too, in the fullness of time…

***

Isabella Linton

Oh my goodness, what a wild and weird creature my sister-in-law has turned out to be.

I remember well the day I first met her. Whatever had possessed her to go cavorting across the moors like that, with that ruffian Heathcliff, straight into the jaws of our dogs? We had to bring her in, of course, after they'd attacked her, but her clothes were torn and stained, her face was filthy, and her hair tangled and matted like an abandoned bird's nest.

Catherine was in a pretty bad way – Skulker's teeth had pierced the skin around her ankle, and she was bleeding badly and clearly in a lot of pain. Father called the doctor to attend to her – which meant, of course, that we first had to bathe her and find her some clean clothing. She ended up wearing one of my nightgowns. The doctor dressed her wound and told her that she must rest completely until it was properly healed. Mother and Father insisted that she had to stay at The Grange with us until she was well enough to return to The Heights. Father sent one of the servants to The Heights with a message for her brother, but then the following day he went across there himself and berated Hindley for not keeping his household under better control.

Catherine stayed with us for five weeks in total, during which time her behaviour improved immeasurably. Her appearance also changed for the better; properly groomed and decently clothed, she turned into quite a beauty. By the time she left us, Edgar was totally smitten with her.

When she agreed to marry him, he was absolutely thrilled. And I thought, at least to begin with, that she had a care for him too. She was certainly much more attentive to Edgar after Heathcliff vanished, once she'd got over that dreadful fever she caught just after he disappeared. I've heard that as soon as she discovered he'd gone, she ran out into the rain and stayed out all night, but I don't know if that's true or not. What I do know is that Mother insisted that she should come and convalesce at The Grange. Much good that did all of us; Mother and Father both caught the same fever and were both dead within a few days.

That was three years ago. Edgar and Catherine were finally married two months ago, and they seemed blissfully happy – until last week.

Then that ruffian Heathcliff turned up on our doorstep, right out of the blue. Except that he isn't a ruffian any more. He's turned into a fine gentleman: well-dressed, well-spoken, and with the air of someone who has plenty of money. Nelly didn't recognise him at first. Catherine was beside herself with joy when she saw him, and threw herself into his arms, though Edgar – perhaps not surprisingly – was rather less thrilled at his arrival.

I'm not sure how Heathcliff felt when he saw her. I heard

him tell her that he'd heard about her marriage, though he didn't say when or how he'd found out.

Then he turned to me, and there was a curious look in his eyes. I felt my heart flutter...

***

Edgar Linton

Isabella appears to have developed an unhealthy fascination for Heathcliff. I am seriously worried about this. I have not seen him make any effort to discourage her, and to the best of my knowledge he has never done anything without having some selfish ulterior motive behind it...

***

Isabella Linton

I love Heathcliff – far more than Catherine ever loved Edgar. And he might love me, too, if only she would let him. But when I spoke up and told her this, she just tossed her head and said haughtily that she hoped she had misunderstood me.

She is truly a dog in the manger. She cannot have Heathcliff herself, but she cannot bear the thought of him loving someone else.

***

December 1783

Heathcliff

It is now three months since I returned to The Heights, and Christmas is almost upon us. The weather has been cold, wet and windy, and I heard from Nelly that Cathy has been quite unwell. As a result, I have not been to The Grange for several weeks. But Cathy and Linton have invited both Hindley and myself to join them for Christmas luncheon. I am sure that in both our cases, the invitations were more her doing than his. Linton has almost as low an opinion of Hindley as he has of me, but he would hardly be in a position to refuse hospitality to his own brother-in-law. I have no idea what kind of ruse Cathy would have employed in order to have the invitation also extended to me. Maybe she just did it without telling her husband. That would not have surprised me in the least.

When we arrived at The Grange and Nelly bade us enter, I took the opportunity to enquire after Cathy's health.

"She is much improved, thank you, Mr Heathcliff, considering her condition," Nelly answered – though I could not help but think she appeared a little embarrassed.

Her condition? What could Nelly mean? I was puzzled, but my question was soon answered. As Cathy threw herself into my arms and I held her close, I could not fail to notice the gentle swelling of her belly as it pressed against me.

Recalling what I had learned from John Burgess, I was consumed with jealousy. Here was real proof, if any were needed, that my darling had given Linton what should by rights have been mine. And I wanted that child to be mine. I wanted to watch her grow, month by month, with the fruits of what we've always been to each other.

But as she drew back and looked into my face, I read the message in her eyes. Then I knew I could take some small comfort from the knowledge that, although Linton might have possessed her body, he would never have her heart, her soul or her spirit. Those would remain mine for ever – not merely in this life, but also in whatever might lie beyond.

In the meantime, I must harden my heart yet again. Trelawney's rule has served me well during the past three years. I had hoped I would not need to call upon it again, but it seems that fate has conspired otherwise.

Revenge, I believe, is a dish which is best served cold…

PART FOUR

AFTERMATH

(1784-1802)

Gimmerton, The Yorkshire Moors

January 1784

Heathcliff

Well, that brute Hindley is now well and truly ruined, in more ways than one. Time to put the next stage of my plan into operation...

***

Isabella Linton

Oh, I am so happy! Heathcliff has asked me to marry him. He insists that we must not tell Edgar or Catherine, because they would not approve, so our only option is to elope. He has told me to meet him tonight at the gates of The Grange after everyone else has retired to bed.

How romantic!

***

Heathcliff

It didn't take much to persuade Isabella to run away with me.

We were married yesterday. The silly girl still thought she was in love with me – or rather, she did, until last night. I don't think she'd realised what was in store for her, though in truth I don't believe either of us derived much pleasure from the experience.

For me, it was totally unfulfilling. I now have some idea how my ship-mates might have felt after their nocturnal activities on the slave-ships; a rough coupling, with no affection on either side. Even my experience in the bawdy-house in Baltimore had been more affectionate than this.

As for Isabella, she struggled and screamed throughout – and by this morning she was weeping to go home.

I very much doubt that we will repeat the procedure. But it remains to be seen if it produces any tangible result. I still cannot envisage fathering a child with anyone other than Cathy.

***

Edgar Linton

Isabella has disappeared, and so too has Heathcliff. I fear the worst.

But far more devastating than this is the news that my darling Catherine, who expects our first child in May, is dangerously ill with a brain fever. I cannot imagine how I will cope if I lose her...

***

February 1784

Isabella Linton (now Isabella Heathcliff)

Dear Edgar,
I am now married to Mr Heathcliff. He tells me that we will be returning to Wuthering Heights within a few weeks.
Isabella

Postscript to the above letter, added in pencil in a hurried scrawl:

I most earnestly crave your pardon, dearest brother, if what I have done has caused you any pain or offence. I assure you that I could not help it beforehand, and now that the deed is done, I have no power to retract it.

Please remember me kindly, and I hope that in the fullness

of time you can find it in your heart to forgive me.

Your ever-loving sister.

***

March 1784

Edgar Linton

I am told that Isabella has returned to Wuthering Heights, but I have no wish to see her.

Far better news than this is that at last the fever has turned, and my darling wife is out of danger.

***

Isabella Heathcliff

Dear Nelly,

I wrote to Edgar a little over two weeks since, informing him of my marriage to Mr Heathcliff. I have had no reply, but truth to tell this does not surprise me; I am in no doubt that what I have done must have caused him untold distress.

Mr Heathcliff and I have now returned to The Heights, and I have just heard that Catherine has been very ill. Between this and the pain I must have caused to Edgar, my dear brother must be beside himself with worry.

Oh Nelly, what on earth have I done?

And what on earth have I married? I am seriously beginning to wonder if Mr Heathcliff is even human. If he is, then at the very least he must be mad. But with every day that passes, it seems far more likely that he is the Devil himself.

Now that I come to reflect, I don't think Mr Heathcliff has ever once told me he loves me. And any fanciful notion which I might once have entertained of loving him has long since been crushed.

He shows me no love, no tenderness; just anger and brutality. And as for what happened on our wedding night... I shudder at the memory. I'd always understood it was supposed to be an act of love, but it was so embarrassing and so painful that it felt more like an act of violation. When I awoke the following morning, bruised, torn and sore, I was weeping to go home.

I have been back at The Heights for less than twenty-four hours, Nelly, but already I am miserable beyond endurance. How on earth did you remain sane and cheerful when you lived here, when you had to share your home with such a collection of reprobates? Hindley Earnshaw is constantly drunk, his young son Hareton is like a wild animal (he told me to 'frame off' and threatened to set the dog on me if I did not), and the servant Joseph is coarse and sullen, and most of the time I can barely even make out what he says. The house itself is so cold and uncomfortable, although I could bear those privations if they were the only challenges I must face. But far worse than these is the coldness and hardness in Mr Heathcliff's heart – if indeed he has one.

My own heart returned to The Grange only hours after I left, and, in truth, it is there still; I only wish the rest of me could follow it. I keep hoping that, one day, I will wake up again in my old room, and find that the past two months have been no more than a hideous nightmare.

I know you told me in the past, Nelly, about how Hindley began drinking heavily after his wife had died. But on seeing him again, I now begin to wonder if he is in fact on the verge of madness. A few days ago, he showed me a vicious-looking weapon (a pistol with a double-edged spring knife attached to the barrel) which he keeps concealed in his waistcoat, and said that if he ever found Mr Heathcliff off his guard, he would not hesitate to use it. When I asked why, he ranted and raved about having "lost all, with no chance of retrieval", and declared, "I *will* have it back, and his money, and his blood, and Hell can have his soul." I am still not sure exactly what Hindley meant by this, but after such an outburst I was afraid to be in the same room with him.

How I wish I could turn back the clock. I am now more convinced than ever that not only has my husband never loved me, he has also never ceased loving Catherine. He blames Edgar for her illness, and has declared that he will punish him for what he has done.

But why? Edgar truly loves Catherine, and would never wish for any harm to come to her.

Be that as it may, Mr Heathcliff also says that in the meantime, until he can lay his hands on Edgar, I will suffer on my brother's behalf. I have no idea what he has in mind, but the very thought fills me with dread.

Oh Nelly, I have been such a fool. What I now realise was nothing more than a stupid infatuation has become my own undoing. Please come and visit me; I am so desperate for even the smallest amount of kindness and friendly company. And please tell Edgar that although I fully understand why he is so angry with me, I should dearly love to see him again.

Isabella

***

Nelly Dean

I relayed Miss Isabella's message to Mr Edgar, but although he did not forbid me to visit her myself, he said he still had no wish to see her or to send her any form of communication.

I was surprised and shocked at his coldness towards his sister, and these thoughts troubled me deeply as I made my way to The Heights. As I approached, I observed Miss Isabella peering through the window, as though she had been looking out for me.

Once inside the house, I was shocked at how much it had changed (and not for the better) since I had moved to The Grange. Previously cheerful and homely, it was now gloomy and neglected. Miss Isabella herself looked wan, listless, and slatternly. Mr Heathcliff, on the other hand, had the air of a born and bred gentleman. Indeed, he was the only thing about the house that appeared in any way decent. He greeted me in a friendly manner and invited me to sit down. There was no sign of Hindley.

Miss Isabella (I suppose I should now call her Mrs Heathcliff, but I cannot think of her as such) held out her hand, clearly expecting me to give her the anticipated letter from Mr

Edgar. I shook my head, and immediately sensed her disappointment, so in an attempt to soften the blow, I told a white lie, saying that her that her brother sent her his love and his wishes for her happiness, but that he believed it would be better if there were no further communication between their two houses. She said nothing in response, but as she returned to her seat I saw her lip trembling, as though she were on the verge of tears.

Mr Heathcliff took no further notice of her. Instead he turned his attention to me, and plied me with questions about Mrs Linton's condition. I told him that she was now out of danger but by no means fully recovered, and advised him, out of regard for her health, to make no attempt to see her. Another encounter between him and Mr Edgar would probably be the end of her.

"In that case," Mr Heathcliff retorted, "I shall ensure that I see her only when he is absent. And you, Nelly, will be my accomplice."

I protested, as did Miss Isabella. Mr Heathcliff's response to that was to seize her and thrust her from the room. On returning, he repeated his intention to visit Mrs Linton. Again I refused to assist him – whereupon he threatened to keep me a prisoner at The Heights until I agreed.

What could I do but accept?

***

Heathcliff

My darling Cathy,
I was distraught to learn that you have been so ill. Please allow me to visit you and reassure myself that you are on the road to recovery, and to see if there is anything I can do to help you.

I am entrusting this letter to Nelly Dean to deliver to you. Please send your reply by the same means.

Your ever-loving
Heathcliff

***

It was a full three days before I had the opportunity to deliver Mr Heathcliff's letter to Mrs Linton. On that day, a Sunday, I took it to her room after the remainder of the household had departed for church.

At first, Mrs Linton appeared not to understand the content of the letter; she merely pointed to the signature as though it had awoken some long-forgotten memory. I knew Mr Heathcliff was waiting in the garden, but before I had a chance to send him any kind of response, he had already made his way into the house.

He crossed the room in two strides, clasped her in his arms, and covered her face with kisses. But when he drew back and looked at her, I could see the pain and anguish in his own eyes.

"Oh, Cathy, my life! How can I bear it?" he wailed.

She appeared to take no note of his despair. "You and Edgar have broken my heart," she said. "You have killed me, Heathcliff, and grown strong on it. How long do you plan to go on living after I am gone? Will you be happy when I am dead and buried?"

"Cathy, you are mad," Mr Heathcliff said, through gritted teeth. "Don't torture me until I'm as mad as you!"

At these words, she became calmer. "I only wish that we can never be parted," she whispered. "I wish I could hold you until we are both dead."

Mr Heathcliff clasped her in his arms again, and held her so tightly that I feared he might crush her to death. She appeared still and insensible, and as I approached to see if she had fainted, he held her even closer and snarled at me like a mad dog. I retreated to the window, from whence I could keep an eye on the church in the distance.

When eventually she stirred, he covered her with caresses, and said wildly, "Why did you despise me, Cathy? Why did you betray your own heart? How do you think I will survive when you are gone? Could *you* go on living when your soul is in the grave?"

Out of the corner of my eye I noticed that the people were

now coming out of Gimmerton church. "The service has finished," I said. "The master will soon be returning."

Mr Heathcliff's response to this was to utter a curse and draw Mrs Linton even closer.

I grew more uncomfortable with each passing minute. It was not long before I saw the servants walking up the garden path. Mr Edgar was not far behind them.

"Sir, you must go," I pleaded.

Mr Heathcliff made as if to leave, but Mrs Linton shrieked, her face full of mad resolution. "No! He will not hurt us. Oh Heathcliff, you must not go!"

"Hush, my darling," Mr Heathcliff whispered, clasping her in his arms again. "I will stay. I'm not afraid of him. If he kills me, I will die happy."

Mrs Linton said nothing. She appeared, once again, to have lost consciousness.

I wrung my hands in despair. We were all done for.

Then Mr Edgar strode into the room.

***

Edgar Linton

My darling wife is dead. Giving birth to our daughter, two months ahead of her time, has killed her.

When I returned from church, that villain Heathcliff was there. When I came into Catherine's room, she was in his arms, but apparently unconscious. Heathcliff passed her inert form to me, telling me – no, ordering me – to attend to her first before speaking to him.

It transpires that he had contrived to visit her during my absence. I have no idea what happened during that meeting, but I am convinced that in her weakened state it can have done her no good whatsoever. I cannot help but wonder if the shock of seeing him might have contributed to this catastrophe.

Why, in Heaven's name, could he not have stayed away and left us in peace?

***

Nelly Dean

At first light I found Mr Heathcliff under an old ash tree in the garden, where he had been waiting ever since Mr Edgar returned. I had been dreading having to tell him the terrible news, but he appeared to know, instinctively, that Catherine had died during the night.

I don't think I've ever seen Mr Heathcliff so distressed, though he made a valiant attempt to conceal it. Poor wretch, I thought; he has a heart, just like any other man – so why does he go to such lengths to hide it?

"Did she mention me?" he asked, brokenly.

"She never regained consciousness after you left," I replied. "She died as quietly as a lamb, and now lies with a sweet, peaceful smile on her face."

"Peaceful?" he shrieked, stamping his foot and groaning. "Why should she be at peace whilst I am left in torment?"

He clenched his fists and howled like a savage beast: "Catherine Earnshaw, may you not rest as long as I am living!"

***

Heathcliff

She's gone. Linton's child has killed her. A puny little girl, born two months too early. Why should that little scrap be allowed to live and her darling mother be taken? WHY?

Cathy is my life and my soul. How can I face the rest of my life without her? How can I live when my soul is in the grave?

I must harden my heart even more. Trelawney's training gave me plenty of practice over the past three years, but until now I never imagined I would still need it...

***

Isabella Heathcliff

Catherine is dead. Edgar is distraught with grief, and Heathcliff has been absent from the house for almost a week. When he returned, Hindley was desperate enough to draw his pistol, but Heathcliff grappled with him and succeeded in wounding him badly with his own weapon. He then picked up a kitchen knife and threw it at me.

I cannot take any more of this. I must flee.

But if my trials were already not more than enough to bear, I now believe I may be with child – the product of that one and only act of violation. I can only hope and pray that the poor creature does not inherit anything from its father…

***

Nelly Dean

We buried Mrs Linton yesterday. The only mourners were Mr Edgar, myself, and other tenants and servants. There was no sign of either Hindley or Mr Heathcliff, and I believe Miss Isabella wasn't even invited. Mr Heathcliff had made his last farewell in secret the day before, when Mrs Linton's coffin was still lying open in the parlour. He had put a lock of his hair into the locket around her neck, after having cast out the lock of Mr Edgar's hair which had previously been placed there. I twisted the two locks of hair together and replaced them both in the locket. She had, after all, loved them both. Let a part of each of them be laid to rest with her.

This evening, when I was sitting in the parlour with the baby after Mr Edgar had retired to his room, Miss Isabella suddenly appeared, soaking wet and freezing cold, having run all the way from The Heights wearing only a light silk dress and thin slippers. She was in a dreadful state: scratched, bruised, and with a deep cut beneath one ear.

Once I had persuaded her to change into warm dry clothes and had seated her by the fire with a cup of tea, she pulled off her wedding ring, smashed it with the poker, and flung it into the flames.

"There!" she said, with a sigh of satisfaction. "That is the last thing of his that I have. I am well rid of it – and of him!"

Then she told me what had happened that had forced her to take such desperate action. When Mr Heathcliff finally returned to The Heights after several days' absence, Hindley attempted to attack him with the pistol she had described in her letter to me. But Mr Heathcliff seized the weapon as it fired, and the knife had sprung back and badly wounded Hindley in the arm. When, a few hours later, during another fit of temper, he threw a kitchen knife at her, she seized the opportunity to escape and run to The Grange, with nothing more than the clothes she was wearing.

"I should dearly love to stay here," she sobbed. "It is my rightful home, and I could try to console Edgar, and help to look after the baby. But I know Heathcliff could not bear to see me living happily, here or anywhere else. So I cannot remain anywhere in this neighbourhood."

"Where will you go?" I asked her.

"I will head southwards," she said. "I will find a place where I am known to nobody, and turn my back on my misery and my mistakes."

With that, she finished her tea, kissed the portraits of her brother and sister-in-law, bade farewell to me, and was driven away in the carriage.

I believe she took up residence somewhere near London. I never saw her again, but once things became more settled, she and Mr Edgar established a regular correspondence. For that, at least, I was grateful.

Some months later, we learned that she had given birth to a son, whom she named Linton. From the very beginning she described him as "an ailing, peevish creature". Neither I nor Mr Edgar were willing to give Mr Heathcliff any news of Miss Isabella, but nonetheless he learned (I presume from the servants' gossip) of the birth of the child. He also ascertained where they were living, but thankfully he made no effort to contact her. He probably hated her too much for that.

"They wish me to hate it too, do they?" he remarked to me, on learning of the child's name.

"I don't think they want you to even know about it," I replied.

He sneered. "Be that as it may, I do know about it. And when I want it, I will have it! They can be sure of that!"

September 1784

Edgar Linton

Hindley Earnshaw is dead, having mortgaged The Heights to that villain Heathcliff in gambling debts.

I wonder what will happen to poor Hareton now?

***

Hareton Earnshaw

Nelly has told me that my father is dead. I don't really understand what that means, except that I won't see him again. I'm not sad about that. I don't believe he ever really cared for me.

But Mr Heathcliff has been kind to me. Today, he took hold of me and smiled, saying, "Now, my bonny lad, you are mine!" He said something else too, but there were difficult words in that and I didn't understand them.

I think it will be fun having him as a new father.

***

Nelly Dean

I am really worried about young Hareton. As we were about to leave the house for Hindley's funeral, Heathcliff lifted the lad on to the table and said gleefully, "Now, my bonny lad, you are *mine!* And we'll see if one tree won't grow as crooked as another, with the same wind to twist it!"

The poor child is only six years old, so the meaning of Heathcliff's words was lost on him. But I understood perfectly what Heathcliff had in mind, so I said that Hareton would be better off coming to live with us at The Grange. Mr Edgar himself had agreed with me on that point, though I sensed that his opinion was occasioned more from a sense of duty to his late wife's nephew than from any personal regard for the boy's welfare.

But Heathcliff was adamant that Hareton should remain at The Heights with him.

"I have a fancy," he said, "to try my hand at raising a child. So tell your master that if he attempts to take Hareton from me, I will replace him with my own son."

After the funeral, I returned to The Grange and relayed this message to Mr Edgar – who, I am sad to say, took no further interest in the matter thereafter.

***

June 1797, London

Isabella Heathcliff

Dearest Edgar,

My health is failing, and I do not believe I will live for much longer. Please will you come and see me? I have much to settle, and I wish to bid you a proper farewell and deliver my son – your nephew – safely into your hands.

When I am gone, please will you take care of him? I do not imagine his father will wish to assume the burden of undertaking his education or welfare.

Your loving sister,
Isabella

***

Edgar Linton

Dear Nelly,

My dear sister departed this life yesterday morning. It transpires that her health began to fail a few months after her disastrous marriage, and since then she has never been completely well.

On her deathbed, she asked me to bring her son home with me and take care of him. We will stay in London until after the funeral, and we expect to return to The Grange one week from now. Please procure suitable mourning clothes for my daughter, and arrange a room and other accommodations for my young nephew.

Sincerely,

Edgar Linton

***

July 1797, Yorkshire

Heathcliff

It's now thirteen years since my idiotic wife ran away. I've had no word from her in all that time, though from servant gossip a few months after she disappeared I learned that she gave birth to a son. As if I didn't already have enough cause to hate her, she named the brat Linton!

News has reached me that she is now dead, and her son is coming back with Edgar Linton to live at The Grange.

Well, I'll soon put a stop to that. It would appear that I am destined to be a father after all. Let us see how much I can turn this to my advantage…

***

Nelly Dean

Mr Edgar has just returned from London with his nephew. Young Miss Cathy made a great fuss of her new cousin, but it is hard to imagine that their births were only a few months apart. They're both twelve years old, but he seems so much more infantile than she is.

It pains me to say so, but the child is hardly an asset to the family. Linton Heathcliff is sickly, effeminate and peevish, and clearly enjoys poor health. Either his mother has spoiled him, or (perhaps as a result of being the issue of a marriage of hate) he has inherited the weaknesses of both his parents. Or maybe both.

But it seems that we will not have to endure his company for much longer. Within hours of their arrival, Joseph appeared with a message from Mr Heathcliff, ordering that the child

132

should forthwith be sent to live at The Heights with his father.

Mr Edgar is not in a position to refuse, so he has agreed to send Linton there in the morning. Though I cannot imagine this arrangement being in any way beneficial to anyone concerned, other than possibly to Mr Heathcliff.

***

Heathcliff

Nelly brought my son over to The Heights today.

What a whining, whey-faced weakling I have sired. I hadn't been optimistic about the brat in any case, but he turned out to be far worse than I'd anticipated. He looks for all the world as though he's been reared on sour milk and snails. Joseph even suggested that Edgar Linton had kept my son at The Grange and sent me his own daughter instead.

And the boy didn't even know that I was his father! He's just like his mother, but without any of her redeeming features – and Heaven knows there were few enough of those. But recalling my presence at the childbirth on the *Mersey Rose*, I derived a certain perverse satisfaction from the thought of the agony his mother must have endured in bringing him into the world.

Nelly urged me to take good care of him. And I will – but only because I know he's the heir to The Grange. I want to make sure he lives long enough to inherit it. After that he can go to Hell for all I care, so long as I own it after him…

***

1798

Nelly Dean

From time to time I have been able to enquire in the village how young Linton Heathcliff is faring. The reports are always in the same vein: that he is weak, peevish and disagreeable.

Young Hareton, meanwhile, is denied schooling and is made to work as an unpaid labourer on the land which is rightly his. He, poor fellow, is the only one in the whole neighbourhood who remains in ignorance of how he has been wronged.

***

March 1800

Nelly Dean

My young mistress was fond of her cousin, and was sorry that her acquaintance with him had been so short. Little did either of us know that this was about to change.

Yesterday was her sixteenth birthday. We've never made any attempt at celebrating her birthday, because it's also the anniversary of her mother's death. Her father always passes the day alone in the library and spends the evening in the churchyard.

On this occasion, Miss Cathy announced that she wished to go for a walk on the moors, and prevailed on me to accompany her. But I was unable to keep up with her stride, and eventually she wandered on to the land belonging to Mr Heathcliff.

In the distance I saw two people accost her, evidently believing her to be a poacher. It was only when I caught up with them that I realised that her two apprehenders were none other than Heathcliff and Hareton.

On learning that she was Mr Edgar's daughter, Mr Heathcliff insisted that we must accompany him back to The Heights so that she could meet Linton again. He instructed young Hareton to escort her back to the house, and the two of us followed behind at a more leisurely pace.

During this walk, Mr Heathcliff told me that his long-term plan was that the two cousins should fall in love and marry. He claimed that he would be doing the girl a favour as she has no expectations, and soundly refuted my suggestion that Miss Cathy would be the heir if her cousin died before her.

I sincerely hope he is wrong. But truth to tell, I found myself extremely disturbed by how much he appears to know about the details of the inheritance.

***

Cathy Linton

Yesterday, I had the best birthday I've ever had.

Nelly and I went for a walk on the moors. I wandered too far and found myself on the neighbouring land, where I met a man who it transpires is the father of my cousin Linton!

I haven't seen Linton for more than three years. His father – Mr Heathcliff – took us back to the house so I could see him again.

Linton has grown so much. He is now taller than I am, and he looks so handsome with his fair hair and blue eyes. I remember Nelly telling me that Linton's mother was Papa's sister, my aunt Isabella. Linton looks a little like Papa, but is not nearly as strong.

There was another young man at the house, but he was quite uncouth and behaved like a servant. He couldn't even read! I was quite shocked when Nelly told me that he was my cousin too!

***

Hareton Earnshaw

A young woman came to the house today. She is very pretty, but very rude. She came to see Heathcliff's son. They both made fun of me because I can't read.

***

Nelly Dean

It breaks my heart to see what has become of young Hareton. His situation is even worse than how I imagined after what I'd learned from Zillah.

Mr Heathcliff has been using the lad as a scapegoat for the way Hindley treated him when they were younger, and is forcing Hareton to work as an unpaid, illiterate labourer on what should by rights be his own land. The sins of the father are definitely being visited upon the child, and the child has done nothing to merit this. His only crime is having the wrong parentage.

What makes it doubly distressing is that Hareton appears to be genuinely fond of Mr Heathcliff. He's almost twenty-two now, but clearly has little or no memory of his own father, and no idea at all about how dreadfully his position has been abused.

Or, indeed, why.

***

Cathy Linton

When Nelly and I returned home, I told Papa that we had been to Wuthering Heights and seen Linton again. But far from being pleased about this, he appeared quite upset.

He told me that Mr Heathcliff had acquired Wuthering Heights by dishonest means, that he had treated Aunt Isabella very badly, and that he hates Papa (though Papa did not explain why). To keep him happy I agreed that I would not see Linton again, but I know Linton is expecting me tomorrow and will be upset if I do not go.

So I will write to him instead. Nelly has forbidden it, but I will find a way.

***

August 1800

Nelly Dean

I've just discovered that Miss Cathy has been corresponding with Linton. For several weeks, they have been sending letters to each other; their postman being a young milk-fetcher from the village.

The foolish girl seems to believe she is in love with her cousin, and he with her. She was mortified when she learned that I had discovered her secret, and pleaded with me not to tell her father. Eventually, we burned the letters, and I sent a final missive to Linton telling him that the correspondence was at an end.

***

October 1800

Cathy Linton

It is now two months since I was forced to stop writing to Linton.

Yesterday, Nelly and I chanced to meet with Mr Heathcliff, who told me that Linton is dying of a broken heart after my letters ceased.

Today, Nelly and I went to Wuthering Heights to visit Linton, but Linton and I quarrelled. I told him that his parents had both hated each other – whereupon he told me that my mother had hated my father and loved his. I find that very hard to believe. I never knew my mother, but I cannot imagine anyone ever loving Mr Heathcliff.

***

November 1800

Hareton Earnshaw

Today, when Miss Catherine called to visit her cousin, I told her that I could now read the words above the door: HARETON EARNSHAW. That's my name. At first I thought she was pleased, but then she asked me to read the numbers that came after the words. But I still can't make those out.

She called me a dunce.

She is very rude and very cruel. I will never be good enough in her eyes.

***

Nelly Dean

Mr Edgar and I have both been quite unwell for the past three weeks. During that time, Miss Cathy tended the two of us most faithfully throughout the day. I am now recovered, but yesterday evening she confessed to me that during our period of sickness she has been spending her evenings visiting Linton at Wuthering Heights.

She told me, too, that Hareton had tried to impress her by reading the words inscribed above the door (his own name, *Hareton Earnshaw*), but she called him a dunce because he couldn't also read the figures alongside it (the date, 1500). I had to remind her that he is just as much her cousin as is Linton Heathcliff, and that as a child he had been just as quick and intelligent as she was – and would be still, if Mr Heathcliff had not brought him down so low.

She asked me not to tell her father of her secret visits to The Heights, but I decided that it was better that he should know – upon which he forbade her to visit The Heights again. She wept and wailed, and in an attempt to console her, he promised to write and invite Linton to visit them at The Grange. But with hindsight, I believe that if he had been fully aware of the precarious state of his nephew's health, he might well have withdrawn even that small concession.

***

September 1801

Cathy Linton

A few days ago, Nelly and I met Linton on the moors, and I must own that we were both shocked at how ill he looks. When we met him again today he persuaded us to go back to the house with him, then told me that we will be married in the morning because his father is afraid that he will die soon.

***

Nelly Dean

Mr Heathcliff kept Miss Cathy and me at The Heights for almost a week, during which time he forced her to marry Linton.

After learning from Zillah that Mr Edgar is not long for this world, I returned to The Grange after succeeding in escaping from The Heights. But Miss Cathy is still held prisoner there.

***

Heathcliff

My revenge is almost complete! Edgar Linton's daughter is now married to my pathetic excuse for a son. The puny wretch isn't expected to live much longer, and I've made sure he has signed a will leaving all his property (which naturally includes all of hers) to me. Edgar Linton took what was rightfully mine. Soon, I will legally own everything that was his.

I do wish, though, that he hadn't named the girl after her mother. And that the girl didn't have her mother's eyes. Most of the time, I can hardly bear to look at her – let alone be constantly reminded that her very existence was the reason for my darling's death...

***

Edgar Linton

I know that I have very little time left to live, and I am seriously worried about what might happen after I am gone.

At last, I have realised what that villain Heathcliff has been plotting. Not content with stealing my wife's heart then stealing my sister, he then stole The Heights from my brother-in-law, and now he plans to steal my own home and fortune.

Heathcliff has forced my darling daughter to marry his son in order to gain control of her inheritance, He is now keeping her prisoner at The Heights. I am not even sure if I will see her again this side of the grave, but I must send for the attorney forthwith. I know I can do nothing about The Grange (as it is entailed and hence must pass to young Linton as the eldest male heir), but I need to change my will so that Cathy's fortune is not left directly to her, but rather should be held in trust for her and then for any children she might have. As it is, anything she owns, or will own in the future, is now the legal property of her husband.

If I can achieve that before I leave this world, I should be able to keep her money, at least, out of Heathcliff's grasp if Linton dies...

***

Cathy Linton (now Cathy Heathcliff)

My darling Papa is dead. I persuaded Linton to help me escape so that I could be with him in his final moments.

His last words were, "I am going to her, and you, darling child, shall come to us."

What will become of me now?

***

Nelly Dean

Poor Mr Edgar is dead.

Young Miss Cathy succeeded in reaching her father's bedside just before he left us. This, it transpired, had been with help of her husband, whom she had persuaded to secretly release her from the room where she had been confined. She escaped from The Heights, under cover of darkness, by means of her mother's bedroom window and the fir tree just outside it.

But sadly, Mr Edgar did not succeed in changing his will as he had wished. The attorney had received his message, but instead of coming straight to The Grange, he first called at The Heights to consult Mr Heathcliff. The latter bribed him to delay visiting The Grange until it was too late.

After Mr Edgar's funeral, Mr Heathcliff told me he is seeking a tenant for The Grange, and wants me to stay on there as housekeeper.

Then a queer smile appeared on his face. He said that the previous day, he had visited the churchyard and seen the sexton digging Mr Edgar's grave (alongside that of his wife, on the slope in the corner of the churchyard). When Mrs Linton's coffin was exposed, he opened it.

"Her face is still the same as it always was, Nelly," he said. "I could have stayed there for hours gazing at it, but the sexton told me not to let the air touch it for too long or it would start to change. So I covered her over again, but knocked one side of her coffin loose (not Linton's side, of course!), and told the

140

sexton that when I am buried beside her, the panel must be removed. And the side of my own coffin too – I'm going to have it specially made – so that her dust and mine can freely mingle until no one can tell us apart."

I was shocked. "That was a wicked thing to do, Mr Heathcliff. She is dead. Were you not ashamed to disturb her?"

"Disturb her?" he snarled. "Not in the least. On the contrary – it is she who has disturbed me, night and day, for these past seventeen years! I know she is there, constantly, yet she always remains just out of my sight and just beyond my grasp. Can you imagine what a torment that is?"

This perplexed me; I have never believed in ghosts, and I suspect that the torment he described was no more than a vivid and long-lasting memory.

Be that as it may, Mr Heathcliff has certainly never been the same since he returned from his three-year absence – and I have never ceased wondering what could have happened during that time to have changed him so. I don't suppose I will ever know. Even if I dared to ask, I very much doubt that he would tell me.

But his animosity towards his new daughter-in-law appears to know no bounds. The sickly and feeble young Linton followed his uncle to the grave within a matter of weeks, having first made a will bequeathing all his (and what had been her) property to his father. Poor Miss Cathy is now living at The Heights, widowed, friendless and destitute – and there is nothing I or anyone else can do to help her.

***

October 1801

Charles Lockwood

My new landlord, Mr Heathcliff, appears to be a very strange man, even more misanthropic than I am. Indeed, alongside him I feel positively sociable by comparison.

He has the striking eyes, swarthy skin and dark hair which one would normally associate with a gypsy, yet he is clearly not without means, being the owner of two imposing properties: Thrushcross Grange (of which I am the new tenant) and his own home, Wuthering Heights.

In addition to Mr Heathcliff, the Wuthering Heights household appears to consist of four other people: Cathy (a pretty but miserable young woman, who Mr Heathcliff explained is his recently-widowed daughter-in-law), Hareton (a boorish young man who could be quite handsome if he took care of his appearance), Zillah (a stout and matronly housekeeper), and Joseph (a morose, sinewy old servant whose speech is barely comprehensible). There is also a motley collection of unfriendly dogs, who are clearly not used to the presence of visitors.

But even stranger than Mr Heathcliff is the atmosphere at the house, as I discovered when I found myself obliged to stay there overnight, when a sudden indisposition during my second visit prevented my returning to The Grange. The housekeeper Zillah showed me to a chamber in the attic, which had evidently not been in use for quite some time. She whispered to me as we made our way upstairs that Mr Heathcliff had "an odd notion" about the room, and had never willingly allowed anyone to sleep in it. When I asked the reason, she replied that she did not know. But she had only been living at Wuthering Heights for a year or two, and there were so many "queer goings-on" in the house that she did not know where to begin wondering about them.

At the time it did not occur to me to wonder why Zillah had given me this particular room, in specific defiance of Mr Heathcliff's instructions. But afterwards, I began to appreciate (though not necessarily understand) why my host appeared to have such strong feelings about it.

The room itself was sparsely furnished, containing only a chair, a cupboard, and a large oak closet. The latter, on closer inspection, proved to be an elaborate type of enclosed bed, at one end of which was a small window to the outside world. The window-ledge was home to a few mildewed books, and the painted sill was covered with a handwritten collection of names repeated over and over again: *Catherine Earnshaw*,

Catherine Heathcliff, and (once or twice) *Catherine Linton.*

I found it difficult to sleep at first, so picked up one of the musty-smelling books and began to read it. The fly-leaf bore the words *Catherine Earnshaw, Her Book, 1777,* and the contents proved to be a kind of diary which described scenes of serious domestic discord. Mention was made of Heathcliff (presumably the same Mr Heathcliff who was now my landlord) and also Joseph, who by Catherine's account appeared to have been every bit as surly then as he is now.

I drifted off to sleep, but was troubled by strange dreams – the second of which was so vivid that I was almost convinced it was real. I could hear the strong wind howling through the fir-tree just beyond the window, and the persistent tapping of a branch on the glass outside. The window-handle would not move, so I broke the pane and reached out to break off the offending bough – but instead my fingers were grasped by a small icy hand which would not let go. A plaintive voice repeatedly cried, "Let me in!" and announced its owner to be Catherine Linton.

Linton? What on earth had made me think of Linton rather than Earnshaw (or even Heathcliff)? But whoever she was – Earnshaw, Heathcliff or Linton – Catherine seemed determined to force her way in through the window.

I screamed aloud. My cries must have awoken my host, for within a few moments he appeared in the doorway, but my presence in the room appeared to agitate him even more. It was only after I recounted the details of my nightmare, and begged his pardon for having disturbed him, that he appeared to calm himself a little. He told me to pass the remainder of the night in his own room, as he would be unable to go back to sleep after being thus disturbed.

I made my way out of the room, leaving him inside. But as soon as I had passed through on to the landing, I heard him beat his fist on the window, burst into tears, and wail, "Cathy, my heart's darling, please come in!"

I am beyond baffled. I know that my ghostly apparition was no more than part of a hideous nightmare; this was confirmed by the fact that the window I had broken in my dream was

143

intact when I awoke. But Mr Heathcliff evidently believes in the real existence of the spirit (whatever it might represent), and even appears to actively seek its company.

I believe that my housekeeper at The Grange, Mrs Dean, may know something of the history of this strange family. I will ask her at the first opportunity.

***

Nelly Dean

Mr Heathcliff now has a new tenant for The Grange, a Mr Charles Lockwood. Mr Lockwood has paid a couple of visits to The Heights, and the second time he fell ill and found himself obliged to stay there overnight. When he returned to The Grange he was full of curiosity about the people at The Heights.

I will tell him, of course, since he has expressed an interest...

***

Charles Lockwood

Mrs Dean told me how Mr Heathcliff had first been brought, as a small child, to Wuthering Heights by old Mr Earnshaw, who had found him wandering the streets of Liverpool, ragged and starving.

The Earnshaw children, Hindley and Catherine, were at first most unwelcoming to the newcomer. Catherine's aversion to Heathcliff soon disappeared, but Hindley's grew stronger by the day, and the situation only improved when Hindley was sent away to school. After that, Heathcliff and Catherine were inseparable.

After old Mr Earnshaw died, Hindley returned to Wuthering Heights, with a wife who gave birth to a son (Hareton, the boorish young man I had met during my visit) and who died soon afterwards. Hindley never got over her death and began drinking heavily.

Catherine, meanwhile, became friendly with the children

from Thrushcross Grange: Edgar and Isabella Linton. Eventually, Edgar asked Catherine to marry him and was thrilled when she accepted, though Catherine herself confessed to Mrs Dean, within hours of doing so, that she had doubts about her decision. She told Mrs Dean that her soul was troubled, but that she could not marry Heathcliff because to do so would degrade her.

Mrs Dean believes that Heathcliff must have overheard what Catherine said, because that night he disappeared and was not seen again for three years. But a couple of months after Catherine had married Edgar and they had all moved to The Grange, Heathcliff suddenly reappeared – much improved in manners, appearance and status. Mrs Dean says she has no idea what he did or where he went during those three years, or indeed how he obtained his fortune; in truth, she had never dared to ask.

After Catherine died giving birth to her daughter (Cathy, the young widow I had met at Wuthering Heights), Heathcliff was totally devastated. According to Mrs Dean, immediately after her death he declared: "Catherine Earnshaw, may you not rest as long as I am living!"

***

Nelly Dean

I do hope poor Mr Lockwood isn't too alarmed by what I've been telling him. Personally, I find it very hard to believe all this talk of ghosts. I've never seen one myself, nor do I ever expect to. In the case of Mr Heathcliff, I'm convinced it must all be in his mind. He was never the same after Mrs Linton died.

***

Charles Lockwood

In the years that followed Catherine's death (Mrs Dean continued), Mr Heathcliff became a bitter and cold-hearted man. Mrs Dean believes that he never forgave Hindley Earnshaw for the way he'd treated him when they were children, and seemed hell-bent on revenge. He took full advantage of Hindley's fondness for drinking and gambling, and by the time Hindley died a few months later, the latter had mortgaged The Heights to Heathcliff in gambling debts. Hindley's young son Hareton, who should by rights have inherited the house and land, was now reduced to no more than an uneducated and unpaid labourer – as Heathcliff himself had been when Hindley became master of Wuthering Heights after old Mr Earnshaw died.

Shortly before Catherine died, Edgar's sister Isabella developed an infatuation with Heathcliff – something of which he also took full advantage. He felt no affection for her whatsoever, but seeing the opportunity to use her as a means of avenging himself on Edgar, he persuaded her to elope with him. The marriage was doomed to failure from the start, and one night (following a serious confrontation between Heathcliff and Hindley, during which Isabella herself was injured) she escaped and ran away to London. A few months later she gave birth to a son, Linton Heathcliff.

Isabella died when Linton was twelve, after which Edgar brought the boy (a sickly effeminate child) back to Yorkshire. In the fullness of time, Heathcliff contrived for the dying Linton to marry young Cathy in order to gain control of her property.

Heathcliff's revenge was complete. He had control of Wuthering Heights (revenge on Hindley for what he perceived as past wrongs) and control of Thrushcross Grange (revenge on Edgar for depriving him of Catherine).

All this time, Mrs Dean said, Heathcliff had claimed to be haunted by the ghost of Catherine Earnshaw – the same spirit who had visited me in the attic room at Wuthering Heights. On a later occasion he told her how, the day after Catherine's funeral, he even went so far as to try to dig up her corpse, but was stopped only when he heard her ghost above him in the churchyard.

"Queer goings-on" indeed…

January 1802

Nelly Dean

Mr Lockwood has now left The Grange and returned to his home in London. Zillah has quit her position as housekeeper at The Heights, and Mr Heathcliff has asked me to take her place. At least now I should be able to keep an eye on Miss Cathy – and possibly Mr Hareton as well. They both need all the friends they can get.

***

February 1802

Cathy Heathcliff

Life is a little better now that Nelly has come to live with us, and she has her own parlour which is a haven of peace for both of us. She's even managed to smuggle some of my books over from The Grange. But I do still feel lonely when she has to attend to her housekeeping duties. Sometimes I even go down to the kitchen just for company, although the only ones there are Joseph and Hareton. They both hate me, but even this is better than being totally alone.

***

March 1802

Hareton Earnshaw

I don't know why my cousin comes to the kitchen so often. She doesn't like Joseph, and she doesn't think I'm fit to wipe her shoes.

***

April 1802

Cathy Heathcliff

I realise now that I've treated Hareton very badly. He once tried to teach himself to read, but when I laughed at him, he gave up and burned all his books. At the time I thought that was a very silly thing for him to do, but I see now that I was wrong to laugh at him. He must have been trying to better himself, so he perhaps he isn't such a dunce after all.

And he is my cousin. I must find a way of showing him that I'm sorry and I want to be friends.

***

Nelly Dean

A strange thing happened this evening. Miss Cathy told Mr Hareton that she's glad he's her cousin. At first, he seemed angry, then embarrassed – as though he didn't know how to react. Then she made him a present of one of her books, with the promise if he accepted it she would teach him how to read it.

By the end of the evening they both looked happier than I have seen either of them appear for a long time. I hope this proves to be the start of something good for both of them.

***

Hareton Earnshaw

My cousin has given me a beautiful book and has promised to teach me how to read it properly. I think perhaps she does like me after all. This makes me very happy.

And I do want to learn. I don't want her to go on thinking of me as a dunce.

***

May 1802

Nelly Dean

What a change in Mr Hareton! Years of ignorance and degradation have swiftly given way to intelligence, honesty and warmth – and even his appearance has improved beyond measure.

The only thing which has not altered is his fondness for Mr Heathcliff. Even Miss Cathy has been unable to change his mind about that.

***

Heathcliff

Those two youngsters seem to have become friends. It made me angry at first, but now it's hardly worth the effort. Having finally got my revenge, I find I've lost my appetite for it.

In any case, they seem to avoid me most of the time.

But there is one who won't desert me. By God, she's relentless. All I want now is to be with her.

***

September 1802

Nelly Dean

Mr Lockwood has returned to Yorkshire for a short visit. I think he will be in for a great surprise. So much has happened here since he left…

***

Charles Lockwood

In January of this year, I terminated my tenancy of Thrushcross Grange and returned to London. But on recently finding myself once again in the vicinity of Gimmerton during a visit to a friend in the north, I decided on a whim to pay another call to my former home.

When I arrived at The Grange I found a new housekeeper was in residence, who informed me that Mrs Dean was now living at Wuthering Heights. On making my way there, I was astounded to see Cathy and Hareton (the latter now transformed into a handsome and well-dressed young gentleman) together, and apparently happily so. She was teaching him to read. She called him 'dunce' when he made a mistake, but I could tell from her tone that this was a jest rather than an insult, and he seemed to take no offence.

I found Mrs Dean in the kitchen. She greeted me warmly, and explained that very soon after I had departed for London, Zillah had quit her position as housekeeper at The Heights and that Heathcliff had summoned Mrs Dean to come and take her place.

Her next words took me totally by surprise. Heathcliff had died four months earlier. He had, as she described it, "a queer end".

During the spring months, Cathy and Hareton had gradually become friends. This annoyed Heathcliff immensely at first, but then his behaviour changed in a way which no one could understand. He took long walks alone, refused food, and appeared to see things which were invisible to anyone else. Mrs Dean told me that sometimes she overheard him speaking aloud although she knew there was no one else in the room, and the only word she could make out was "Catherine". His strange demeanour frightened her, and she was afraid to be alone with him – as indeed were all the other members of the household.

At this, Heathcliff said, "Well, there is one who won't shrink from my company! By God, she's relentless."

Then he locked himself in the chamber with the oak-panelled bed (where I had experienced the ghostly encounter). There he remained for the next two nights and the whole day in between. At dawn the following day, Mrs Dean observed from the garden that the window of the room was swinging open, and she found another key to open the chamber door.

She found Heathcliff lying on the bed, open-eyed and apparently smiling, but stone-cold dead.

They buried him quietly, with his coffin, and that of Catherine, both open-sided as he had ordered, although it scandalised the whole of the neighbourhood. The only one who appeared to lament his passing was young Hareton – ironically, the one whom he had most wronged.

Freed from their oppressor, Cathy and Hareton grew closer still, and are now planning to marry. After their wedding they and Mrs Dean will move to The Grange. Joseph will remain at The Heights, possibly with a lad for company (I only hope he can understand the old man's speech better than I ever could). They will live in the kitchen, and the remainder of the house will be shut up. Such ghosts as wish to inhabit the place can thus roam free and undisturbed.

Mrs Dean says she believes the dead are at peace, but I am not so sure…

***

Nelly Dean

It's been four months since Mr Heathcliff died, and Miss Cathy and Mr Hareton are now inseparable. Peace has at last been restored, and I am very much looking forward to their wedding on New Year's Day. Then we can return to The Grange and leave this gloomy house for ever.

But something happened this evening which has left me very puzzled. On returning to The Heights from a trip to Gimmerton, I encountered a young shepherd-boy trembling and crying by the side of the road. When I asked him what was troubling him, he sobbed that he'd seen "Heathcliff and a woman" on the moors.

Poor young thing, I thought. I comforted him as best I could, telling him that there are no such things as ghosts, and that the stories he's heard about them are precisely that: stories, and nothing more. But neither he nor his sheep would go any further across the moors, so I told him to go round by the road.

It was only after I returned to The Heights, and chanced to glance across the moors towards The Grange, that I heard voices in the garden – a man's and a woman's. Ah, I thought, Miss Cathy and Mr Hareton are coming back from their walk. But when I entered the kitchen, I found the two of them seated by the fire, reading a shared book. They both confirmed that neither of them had left the house for the whole day, and that nobody had called during my absence.

I dashed back to the door and peered out. Beneath the oak tree stood two shadowy figures, locked in a passionate embrace.

As they drew apart and emerged into the pale moonlight, I had full sight of them. The man was tall and well-built, with craggy features and jet-black hair turning grey at the temples. He appeared to be some fifteen or twenty years older than his companion: a slight young woman with pale skin, long brown hair, and striking dark eyes.

What was it Mr Lockwood said? "Queer goings-on..."

I think he may well have been right.

Epilogue

This letter was found concealed in the oak closet bed at Wuthering Heights after Heathcliff's death. Alongside it was Heathcliff's clay pipe, which Nelly had found in the kitchen the night Heathcliff disappeared. It is not known if Heathcliff ever knew of the letter's existence.

My darling,

Why did you leave us? Where have you gone? I am frantic with worry about you.

Nelly told me that you had overheard our conversation about my decision to marry Edgar Linton. Or, at least, that you'd heard the first part of it, and that you left when you heard me say that it would degrade me to marry you.

Oh, my dearest, if only you had stayed to hear more, you would have known that I love you more than life itself. I cannot imagine a life without you. It would not be a life; it would be no more than a miserable, pointless existence.

You are always in my heart and in my soul. My love for Edgar will change with time, but my love for you is as eternal as the rocks beneath the moors.

Did I ever tell you that I once dreamed that I had died and gone to Heaven? But I was so unhappy there that the angels threw me out. I came back to earth and landed right on the top of Wuthering Heights. That is my true home, in body, mind, and spirit, and will be for ever – with you.

Why on earth did I ever say it would degrade me to marry you? What a stupid, ignorant, selfish fool I was. Whatever our souls are made of, yours and mine are the same. It is as though we were cast from the same mould.

If I should die before you, my darling, I will never leave you. I will stay with you on earth until we can be together for all eternity.

I will love you for ever. Please come back to me.

Catherine

***

Another letter found hidden in an old deed-box discovered in an attic at Wuthering Heights, some years after Heathcliff's death:

I know that my days are now numbered, and I cannot go to face my maker without unburdening myself of this secret which I have kept for my whole life. I cannot speak of this to anyone, so now my only recourse is to write the story down.

Back in 1763, when I was visiting Liverpool for business, I foolishly became drawn into the company of ladies of the night. One of them was a particularly comely wench, with long thick black hair and striking eyes. She told me that her name was Mary O'Keefe, and that her family were Irish gypsies who had fled from their homeland some years earlier, when the crops had failed and the people were starving. She described the time as the 'years of slaughter'. On arriving in Liverpool, she had tried and failed to find respectable employment, and had eventually succumbed to the oldest profession of all.

I am not proud of what I did. This is the one and only time when my attentions have strayed. My wife had been gravely ill following the birth and subsequent death of our son Heathcliff, and our marriage bed was cold for many months thereafter.

I spent but one night with Mary, and gave the matter no further thought apart from periodic vain attempts to salve my conscience. Then, a few years later, I had reason to return to Liverpool, and found a dark-haired boy wandering the streets. He looked no more than four or five years old, but he was dirty, starving, dressed in rags, and barely able to speak except in grunts.

I thought of my own children, and realised that they, but for the grace of God, could also be homeless and hungry. I decided there and then to give this poor child a proper home.

"He is a gift from God," I said to my wife, when I arrived back at The Heights. "And we shall name him Heathcliff, after our own dear departed baby son."

But my wife clearly did not share my enthusiasm for the new arrival. "Another brat to rear, and another mouth to feed," she grumbled. "And how do you think Hindley and Catherine will accept this cuckoo in the nest?"

My wife's fears were not unfounded. Both children were furious that the gifts I had promised them (a fiddle for Hindley and a whip for Catherine) had been damaged or lost as a direct result of my attention to the foundling. And even Nelly appeared to take an instant dislike to the child. It took quite some time for life at The Heights to return to some semblance of normality.

Hindley was wildly jealous of the newcomer, and domestic harmony was only fully restored after he went away to college. Catherine, on the other hand, soon forgot her initial aversion to Heathcliff, and it was not long before the two of them were completely inseparable. Indeed, they seemed like soulmates. So much so that it would not surprise me in the least if, in the fullness of time, they should decide to marry.

It was only some years later, as Heathcliff grew into a tall and striking young man, that I noticed that he had developed an uncanny resemblance to Mary as I remembered her. I will never know for certain, but now I cannot help wondering if Heathcliff could have been the product of my one and only marital indiscretion. In which case, as I can tell no one on earth of my concern, I can only hope and pray that neither he nor Catherine will ever find out the truth…

Samuel Earnshaw
September 1777

THE END

Author's Note

It all began with a chance remark from a former schoolfriend:

"Sue, I love the way you've based your book on what we did at school. What are you going to do next?"

We were chatting just after the release of my third novel, *The Unkindest Cut of All*, which features a performance of Shakespeare's *Julius Caesar*. This was the play we'd studied for English Literature O-Level (as it then was, back in the dark ages before GCSEs). The novel set for the same exam was Emily Brontë's classic *Wuthering Heights*.

"Well," I chuckled, "there's always Heathcliff…"

At the time, it was just a passing joke between two friends who recalled crying on each other's shoulders as we'd struggled to make sense of the vagaries of the plot, tried (and mostly failed) to decipher Joseph's incomprehensible dialect, and attempted to understand the book's complicated inter-personal relationships. The latter was not made any easier by the characters' confusing similarity of names. Emily Brontë had clearly never read the rule-book about this. Three of the characters have names beginning with the same initial, one of them has a first name which is the same as the surname of another, and two others have the same name entirely!

But somehow, the idea just wouldn't go away. I then recalled how our teacher (the wonderful Mrs Hall) explained how *"…by having the story narrated by Nelly Dean, Emily Brontë avoids having to tell us exactly what happened to Heathcliff during those missing three years…"*

So – what might have happened to him? Could I try to get into his mind, and write a story which attempts to answer that question?

It proved to be quite a challenge, as the dates in *Wuthering*

Heights are very precise. Heathcliff disappears from 1780 to 1783. My first idea was that he could have spent his missing years as a pirate (which would certainly be in keeping with his character!), but I quickly discovered when I started my research that the golden age of piracy was several decades too early. Then I wondered if perhaps he could have made his fortune in the American or Australian goldrush, but the goldrush years were not until the mid-1800s. That left me with just two options which did fit with the correct dates: smuggling and slavery.

Smuggling was very common in coastal areas all around Britain in the 18th and 19th centuries, and was seen as fair game by rich and poor alike. The practice evolved in response to punitive taxes imposed by a series of governments, each more desperate than its predecessor, who needed the money to pay for costly wars in Europe and America. Whole communities took part in the trade, and everyone profited from it.

It was whilst researching the history of smuggling that I came across the inn which provided the inspiration for The Mermaid: Old Mother Redcap's at Wallasey (on the opposite side of the Mersey estuary from Liverpool). In the 18th century, this was a centre for smuggling, and also a haven for sailors trying to avoid the press gang. It was full of clever hiding places where contraband – or people – could be concealed. There was also a trap door situated directly behind the front door. If the door was forced, this would automatically operate the bolt of the trapdoor, and the intruders would fall into the cellar (around 8-9 feet below). Mother Redcap herself was a lady named Poll Jones, who always wore a red cap or bonnet. She was a great friend to sailors and smugglers, and even looked after their money whilst they were away at sea.

The practice of using food to conceal illicit goods (such as wine, spirits and sugar) was quite common in the 18th and 19th centuries. Recipe books from the time reflect this: soups were enhanced by the addition of wine, sherry or Madeira, stews used whole bottles of wine (rather than just a few spoonfuls), whilst cakes and puddings were often enriched with rum or brandy. This suggests that having large quantities of alcohol on the premises could have been difficult to explain if the revenue men came calling, so the liquor had to be consumed quickly to avoid detection. Be that as it may, in any case it would certainly have helped to liven up the drab everyday diet of the time.

John Burgess's trial is based partly on a real event. The prevailing winds along the south-west coast of the Isle of Anglesey caused many shipwrecks, but in some cases the wrecks were not accidental. The wreckers and robbers of Crigyll, near Rhosneigr, lured ships on to the rocks at night using lanterns and beacons which simulated the harbour lights of Holyhead, a few miles to the north. Once the ships were scuppered, the robbers would plunder the wrecks and steal their cargo. The gang was active for over 30 years and proved extremely difficult to convict. Eventually, in the early 1740s, four of the ringleaders were caught and brought to trial at Beaumaris Courthouse, charged with plundering the ship *Loveday and Betty*. But they hired a brilliant lawyer to defend them, the judge was drunk, and other members of the gang surrounded the building and terrorised the jury into returning a verdict of Not Guilty.

For research into the slave trade, I am indebted to the International Slavery Museum in Liverpool (**www.liverpoolmuseums.org.uk/ism/**), which I can highly recommend to anyone who wants to learn more about this grim period of history. By the 1780s, Liverpool was the European capital of the transatlantic slave trade, and was responsible for the movement of around 1.5 million slaves in total. This figure represents more than 10% of all known Africans transported into slavery.

The 'years of slaughter' (which had caused Mary O'Keefe to leave Ireland) refers to the Irish famine of 1740-1741. The country suffered several successive years of extremely cold and wet weather, resulting in disastrous crop failure and mass starvation.

As for Bonnie Prince Charlie ('the King over the Water'), I'm afraid William McDougal's dream of restoring the Catholic monarchy was indeed, as Heathcliff had feared, a lost cause. After losing at the Battle of Culloden in 1746, the Prince spent five months on the run before escaping to France. After secretly converting to Protestantism in an unsuccessful attempt to win the English over to his side, he eventually died in 1788 in miserable obscurity.

In the sections of the book which overlap with the original story, I was forced to take one or two liberties, such as giving putative first names to Mr Lockwood and old Mr Earnshaw. But otherwise I have tried to stay faithful to Emily Brontë's narrative (whilst avoiding, wherever possible, quoting from it directly).

The question of Heathcliff's parentage is another of literature's great mysteries. I hope my suggestion (which tallies, at least in part, with that opined by some Brontë scholars) provides a plausible-sounding explanation. But the hints that his change of personality might have been the result of having contracted syphilis (the pox), which could also have contributed to the early deaths of his wife and son, are purely my own invention.

Sue Barnard
May 2018

Fantastic Books
Great Authors

CROOKED
CAT

Meet our authors and discover
our exciting range:

- Gripping Thrillers
- Cosy Mysteries
- Romantic Chick-Lit
- Fascinating Historicals
- Exciting Fantasy
- Young Adult and Children's
  Adventures
- Non-Fiction

Made in the USA
Columbia, SC
18 June 2018